THE HIDDEN

THE HIDDEN

A NOVEL OF SUSPENSE

BILL PRONZINI

Walker & Company
New York

Published by Walker Publishing Company, Inc., New York

All papers used by Walker & Company are natural, recyclable products made from
wood grown in well-managed forests. The manufacturing processes conform to the
environmental regulations of the country of origin.

LIBRARY OF CONGRESS CATALOGING-IN-PUBLICATION DATA HAS BEEN APPLIED FOR.

ISBN: 978-0-8027-1800-6

Visit Walker & Company's Web site at www.walkerbooks.com

First U.S. edition 2010

1   3   5   7   9   10   8   6   4   2

Typeset by Westchester Book Group
Printed in the United States of America by Worldcolor Fairfield

For two of the best:
Ed Gorman and Tom Piccirilli

ACKNOWLEDGMENTS

I'm indebted to Sam Parsons, former EMT, South Coast VFD, for sharing his expertise.

Thanks also to George Gibson of Walker & Company and my agent, Dominick Abel, for their ongoing support. And to Marcia, for all the usual reasons.

Crime is a fact of the human species, a fact of that species alone, but it is above all the secret aspect, impenetrable and hidden. Crime hides, and by far the most terrifying things are those which elude us.

—Georges Bataille

But how do we recognize ourselves? How can man know himself? He is a dark and hidden thing.

—Friedrich Nietzsche

PROLOGUE

MIDSUMMER–LATE FALL

Midsummer

HE MADE HIS WAY slowly down the steep, winding cliffside path. From there, the curved stretch of beach below looked deserted. Clean white sand studded with scattered chunks and piles of driftwood and dark wormy ribbons of kelp. But there were sheltered places under the long rocky overhang toward the bottom that you couldn't see until you were all the way down.

Clouds shifted away from the moon, and the sand and the slow-breaking waves lit up with a kind of iridescent white glow. A long yellow-white streak appeared on the ocean's surface, extending out over some of the offshore rocks where the gulls nested, giving their limed surfaces a patch-painted look. He paused to take in the view. Nice night. Warmish, not much wind. The tide just beginning to come in. He liked nights like this, quiet, peaceful, empty, as if he had the sea and the scalloped shoreline all to himself.

It took him another five minutes to get to where the path dropped sharply onto the beach. He stood there for a few seconds, scanning the inland curve in both directions and as much as he could see of the bare sand reaching back under the overhang. No sign of anybody. But that was where whoever owned the battered Dodge Charger up on the parking area had to be. There were no other hidden places.

He heard them before he saw them. Sudden whoops of laughter, like rips in the night's stillness. Two people, one male, one female. Young, judging from the laughter and the raised voices that followed it.

The sounds came from the other side of a high, squared-off pile of drift-wood that somebody had built into a skeletal fort, bleached pieces jutting here and there like fragments of splintered bone. He slogged in that direc-tion. When he came around on the inshore side of the fort, he saw them— far back under the overhang, sprawled side by side on a blanket.

They didn't see him until he stepped out of the shadows into the powdery moonshine. The girl let out a little cry and raised an arm to point; the boy lifted himself to one knee. He kept moving toward them, slow, out of the light and into more shadow from the overhang. The boy snapped something up off the blanket—a flashlight. The beam stabbed out, found him and steadied on him. He shielded his eyes with his hand, but still he couldn't see much of either kid behind the glare.

"Hey, man. Who the hell are you?" Wary, but not afraid.

"Lower the light, okay? My eyes are sensitive to glare."

Nothing for a time. Then the shaft dipped some, so that it pinned him from the chest down. His night vision came back and he could see them more clearly. Young, all right, late teens or early twenties. The girl was blonde and chubby, the boy dark and lean with a stubbly growth of whiskers on his chin. On one end of the blanket was a rolled-up sleeping bag, on the other a bottle of wine and two plastic cups. A second bottle, empty, and fast-food bags, napkins, trays, wrappers, half-eaten burgers, and ketchup-smeared french fries lay strewn over the sand behind them. Slobs' party. And wine and food weren't all they were partying with. The light wind carried the faint acrid scent of pot.

He said, "Looks like you're planning to spend the night here."

"So what if we are? What's it to you?"

"No overnight camping on this beach."

The girl giggled. "We didn't see any signs." Stoned, her words slurred.

The boy said, "None of your business anyway, man."

"Maybe it is."

"Yeah? You think so?"

"What about all that trash there?"

"What about it?"

"You going to take it away with you?"

"Screw the trash," the girl said, and giggled again.

"Crapping up the beach," he said. "I don't like that."

"Who cares what you like, man."

"Tell him to go away, Eddie," the girl said.

"You heard her." There was a length of driftwood the size of a baseball bat on the sand next to the blanket; the boy picked it up. "Go away, leave us alone. Find some other place, you want to hang down here."

He looked at them for a time, at the trash again. Then he turned and slogged back around the bone-pile fort and down to the waterline where the sand was firmer and you could walk without shuffling your feet. Thick humps of cloud had slid back over the moon again; the sea and the wet sand gleamed sleek and dark, like tar.

He walked for a ways, watching and listening to the slow-breaking rollers. The night breeze had sharpened and it was cooler here close to the water. Behind him he could hear the two kids whooping it up again, drifting snatches of sound that finally faded into silence.

Ahead, a bleached and gnarled log lay half buried in the sand. He veered over to it and sat on one haunch. Far out to sea, at the lip of the horizon, the lights of a passing ship were visible. He watched the lights until they disappeared to the north, then watched the dark sea. The night was quiet now, except for the low hiss of surf.

But it wasn't the same anymore. They had spoiled it for him by spoiling the beach.

The moon reappeared, shedding its silvery light over the sand and the water. But it just wasn't the same. He got to his feet and walked back the way he'd come, stopping once to examine something that gleamed in the sand—a jagged shard of green bottle glass, sharp enough to cut somebody's foot. He put it into his pocket, then left the wet sand and angled up toward the fort.

When he came around behind it, he could see and hear them back there under the overhang. They were together in the sleeping bag now, screwing; the bag moved and jerked like a live thing and the sounds they were making rolled out at him, grunts from the boy and little animal squeals from the girl. The trash was still strewn out behind them.

They were too busy to hear him approach, didn't know he was there until he walked right up beside them. The girl saw him first out of one half-closed eye; the eye popped wide and she cried out, "Eddie!" and twisted out of the boy's embrace. The boy rolled over, sat up blinking. The sleeping bag wasn't zipped; the flap fell away from their naked torsos and the girl immediately covered her bare breasts with both hands.

"Goddamn it," the boy said, "you scared the shit out of us creeping up like that. What the hell's the idea?"

"You two crapping up the beach," he said, "spoiling it for everybody else. That's the idea."

"Are you nuts? Get outta here!"

"No."

The girl said in her slurry voice, "You better do what Eddie says. He's bigger'n you, man."

"That's right, bigger." The boy leaned out of the bag, caught up the chunk of driftwood again. "You don't haul ass right now, I'll bust your head for you."

"I don't think so," he said.

"Listen, man—"

He drew the 9-mil Glock.

A frightened whimper came out of the girl and he shot her first. Otherwise she might have screamed and he hated to hear a woman scream. He shot the boy as he tried to scramble out of the bag. Head shots, both— clean kill shots. He didn't need to check to make sure they were dead.

But it didn't look right, the way they were lying, the boy sprawled back across the naked girl with one arm flung over her face. Messy, and he didn't like messes. It was a lesson his mother had drummed into him when he was a kid, about the only good lesson he'd ever learned from her. And army discipline had reinforced it later on. Always clean up your messes. So he always did. His, and other people's too.

He put the Glock back into his jacket pocket, picked up and pocketed the ejected shell casings. He nudged the two sprawled bodies around until they were lying side by side in the sleeping bag, pulled the flap up to their chins. Better. Tidier.

Then he began collecting the trash so he could take it with him when he climbed back up the cliffside path.

Early Fall

He sat on the hood of his car, smiling as he watched the sea lions. There were three of them, a fat graybeard and two sleek brownish-tan younger ones. When he'd first driven in along the river, the younger ones were playing in the silty brown water, zooming along on their backs, rolling over and diving and chasing each other. Fun to watch because they were having fun, like puppies or a couple of little kids in a swimming pool. Now all three were up on the sandbar near where the river flowed into the Pacific, the old one lying on his side with his belly exposed, the young ones boxing each other with their flippers.

It was late afternoon, cold and gray, fog already obscuring the river mouth and the beach and parking area where the road ended. There was nobody around except him and the sea lions.

Until the guy on the motorcycle showed up.

He heard the machine's sputtering roar a long way off, knew by the sound of it that it was coming fast along the narrow road. It made a hell of a racket when it came barreling around a bend into sight. The rider geared down and braked hard, smoking his tires as he shot past, then pulled up a short ways ahead and sat there juicing the throttle. The sea lions didn't like the noise any more than he did; they stirred around out on the sandbar, the older one rolling onto his belly and waggling a flipper, then edging closer to the water.

The noise finally quit. The rider, dressed in a black leather jacket and black leather leggings, shoved the kickstand down and took off his helmet; he had long straggly red hair and a matching beard. From one of the saddlebags he produced a flattish pint bottle half full of something that was probably whiskey, unscrewed the cap, and took a long swallow. Smacked and then wiped fat lips, glancing over in his direction.

"Colder'n a witch's tit, eh?"

"Pretty cold," he agreed.

The rider walked out onto the narrow strip of grass and rocks that separated the road from the river's edge. Stopped halfway along, unzipped his fly and urinated onto a bush before continuing to the waterline. Stood for a few seconds looking at the sea lions, then emptied the bottle and hurled it at them. It landed short of the sandbar, making a flat splash. The man picked up a rock and threw that, missing wide; pitched a second rock that narrowly missed the graybeard. All three animals had started a confused barking.

By then he was off the hood and running through the grass. "Hey! Hey, you, don't do that."

A scowl and a red-eyed stare. "Do what?"

"Throw things at those sea lions. You almost hit one."

"Too bad I didn't. I hate those buggers. What's it to you, anyway?"

"Plenty. It's plenty to me."

"Yeah? You want to make something out of it?"

"Yes," he said, "I do."

The cyclist took an aggressive step toward him, one arm lifting, the hand bunching into a fist.

And died that way, without enough time to even look surprised.

He shifted his gaze to the sandbar to see if the noise of the shot had frightened the sea lions.

Damn. They were already gone.

Late Fall

From the trees behind the cabin he watched the old man cutting up tree branches with a chain saw. It was a windy day, and every time there was a fresh gust the harsh whine of the saw grew louder, more shrill. The noise was like needles poking into his ears.

Past where the old man worked sat brush piles and stacks of bigger logs from the trees that had been cut down in the land crease and along the bluff top beyond. The sections were naked now except for scattered stumps like blemishes on the hard earth. Must've been two dozen or more taken down—old-growth pines, maybe some redwoods too like the ones back here where he was hidden. Beautiful trees, the pines heavy with cones, the redwoods thick with burls. In the wind they had a kind of swaying grace that reminded him of dancers moving to the rhythmic beat of music. Ugly music now . . . that damn chain saw.

The old man shut off the racket finally, laid the saw down, and stood flexing kinks out of his back and shoulders. Seventy, at least, but wiry and spry in a lumberman's jacket and a cloth cap. Pretty soon he went over to the cabin, a small place built out of unpainted redwood, and bent to take a drink from a water tap.

Time. He moved slowly out of the woods into the clearing behind the cabin.

The old man was on the way back to the logpile by then. Jerked to a stop, bent forward a little, staring. Startled at first, then puzzled, then guarded.

"Say, where'd you come from?"

"The trees back there," he said.

"This is private property, mister. You're trespassing."

"Sure, I know."

"Well? What do you want?"

"I followed you," he said.

"What you mean, you followed me?"

"From the store in town."

"I ain't been to the store today."

"Not today. Yesterday."

"Yesterday? You been hanging around here since then?"

"Part of the time."

"What the devil for?"

"I heard somebody in the store say you'd been clear-cutting trees. I wanted to find out if it was true."

The old man said, "So it's true. So what?"

"I don't like it when people clear-cut."

"Don't matter what you like, this ain't your property."

"Why did you do it?"

"What difference does that make?"

"I asked you why. The trees weren't dead or diseased, were they?"

"No."

"Healthy trees, then. Why did you cut down healthy trees?"

The old man's seamed face had reshaped into a glower. "Well, hell. Look at that view down the declivity and across the bluff—whitewater view now. You could barely see the ocean before—"

"I thought so."

He took the Glock from his jacket pocket.

The old man said, "Jesus Christ!" and backed up a step, wide-eyed. He hadn't been afraid before. Now he was. "What's that for?"

"What do you think it's for?"

"Listen, all I got on me is twenty bucks and there's nothing in the cabin—"

"I don't want your money."

"God's sake, what then?"

"I told you, I don't like clear-cutting."

"You ain't gonna shoot me—"

"Yes," he said, "I am."

"For cutting down trees? You can't kill a man for that!"

"It's not the only reason," he said, and fired.

BETWEEN CHRISTMAS
AND NEW YEAR'S

ONE

THEY WERE HALFWAY THROUGH the treacherous cliffside section of Highway 1 between Jenner and Fort Ross when the rain started.

Macklin thought, Damn! and flicked on the windshield wipers. It was dark now, just after five, and the twisty two-lane road glistened wetly in the Prius's headlight beams. No other traffic in sight; there'd been only a smattering of cars in either direction since they passed through Jenner.

Beside him, Shelby shifted position and spoke for the first time in nearly half an hour. "I knew it," she said. "I knew this was a bad idea."

"It's only a light drizzle."

"Followed by heavier rain, followed by a storm with high winds, followed by unsettled weather that probably means another storm by New Year's Eve."

"The forecasters aren't always right."

"Want to bet they're not this time?"

Macklin glanced over at her. She was huddled low on the seat, her arms folded under her breasts as if she were cold despite the cranked-up heater. In the shadowy glow of the dash lights she looked younger than thirty-five, the same effect as soft room lights and candlelight. It was only in bright light, harsh light, that the age, worry, and stress lines were evident. The years she'd spent on the ambulance, all the carnage and death she'd seen and had to deal with, were partly responsible. But mainly he was to blame. Twelve years of marriage to him had sucked the youth out of her. And he hated himself for it, even though he'd had damn little control over the process.

"We should have left earlier," she said. "Driving in wet weather in daylight is bad enough. Why didn't you wake me sooner?"

"Three straight night shifts. You needed the rest."

"Five whole days off. I could've slept in the car."

"Okay, I'm sorry. You're right, we should've left earlier."

Silence for a time. Then, "I still think this is a bad idea. I don't see why you're so set on it."

You will soon enough, he thought. "We needed to get away."

"Oh, we did?"

"Just the two of us. We haven't been anywhere alone together in almost two years."

"We're alone together at home. A four-hundred-mile round-trip in the dead of winter just to spend four days in an isolated seaside cottage—it just doesn't make a lot of sense to me."

"Four days free of charge, don't forget that."

"Holiday charity from good old Ben Coulter."

"You know Ben's not that way. He's only owned the cottage a year and a half and he likes having people stay there when he's not using it."

"Must be nice to be rich," Shelby said.

"Ben's not rich, not by today's standards."

"A successful software business, a house in Los Altos Hills, a second home on the Mendocino coast, a daughter in a private school—that's rich by *my* standards."

"Well, anyway, we'll have these next few days to ourselves. At home . . . distractions, interruptions, another dull New Year's party somewhere, friends showing up unannounced—"

"What friends, besides Mary Ellen and John, Ben and Kate?"

"Come on, we have more than that."

"Acquaintances, yes, not what I call friends."

The distinction wasn't worth arguing. "Besides," he said, "we didn't really enjoy Christmas."

"It was all right."

"But not very festive."

"How could it be, the way things have gone this year?"

It wasn't meant as a jab at him, but it might as well have been. The way things had gone this year. Losing his office manager's job when the recession forced Conray Foods to downsize. Not being able to find another, even something blue collar that paid decent wages, because he was overqualified—six months now and counting. Even Ben couldn't help him; he knew nothing about software technology and there were no office staff openings at Coulter, Inc. And now this other thing . . . what would Shelby say if he just blurted it out, right here in the dark car? But he wouldn't. Couldn't. That was why this time alone together was so important, to help soften the blow. Maybe soften it, if the next four days went better than this one had so far.

He said, trying to sound cheerful, "Even if the weather's bad, it'll be nice at the cottage."

"Will it?"

"You've seen the photos. Oceanfront, all the amenities."

"In the middle of nowhere."

"Three miles to the nearest town—hardly the middle of nowhere."

"Town, Jay? With a population of ninety-seven? That's not even a hamlet."

"Remember the driving trip to Oregon? We came back down the coast and you liked the area then, you said it was beautiful up here."

"That was ten years ago. And in the summer, with the sun shining."

He didn't want to argue; that was the last thing he wanted. Best to keep his mouth shut. Shelby's mood was prickly enough as it was.

"You'd better turn the wipers on full," she said. "Your drizzle is turning into a downpour."

The wind-driven rain pelted down with increasing velocity the farther north they traveled. The serpentine coast highway grew slick, runoff puddles forming in low-lying areas along its verges. Macklin lowered his speed to fifty, to half that on some of the sharper curves. The road remained deserted for long intervals; the few cars he saw seemed to be mostly highway patrol and county sheriff's cruisers.

His neck and shoulders had begun to ache a bit. Once he thought of asking Shelby to take over; she was a better driver than him, not so overly cautious in conditions like these. But he didn't do it. He felt all right, not too fatigued. Nothing to be gained in shifting the burden to her.

They passed through a handful of widely spaced little towns and villages, all of which had an abandoned aspect like illuminated ghosts. Hardly any tourists this time of year, on a Sunday in weather like this, and the residents forted up for the night. Most of the roadside businesses were closed, taverns and a few restaurants and lodging places the only ones open. Night-lights, neon signs, leftover Christmas decorations—all shone fuzzy and remote through the curtain of rain.

Macklin checked the odometer again. Not much farther now—another ten miles to Seacrest, the nearest village, and another three beyond that to the cottage. He'd memorized the landmarks and mileage distances Ben had given him, but when they got to Seacrest he'd go through the mental checklist again to make sure he had them all.

Shelby hadn't said a word since their conversation after the rain started. He glanced over at her again. She was sitting motionless, hands resting palms up on her thighs. Asleep? No. Her head moved slightly and in the dash lights he could see the faint gleam of one opened eye. Brooding, maybe, about some of the same things that had been on his mind lately. About the coming New Year, their financial problems, their life together and all that had gone wrong with it.

It wasn't that she was easy to read—everybody had depths that no one else could fathom—but after twelve years he was familiar with her moods and the way her mind worked. Until recently she'd been more or less open about herself, her feelings, her needs and concerns. The exact opposite of him. All his life he'd been a closed book, not only to her and others but to himself. Not by conscious choice; it was as if the pages in the Jay Macklin book were glued down and he couldn't pry them loose no matter how hard he tried.

Part of the reason was his childhood—his weak-willed mother, his coldly indifferent father, the fact that he hadn't made friends easily and wasn't popular, at least not until his high school peers found out just how good a baseball player he was; and even then he'd remained the kind of kid who mostly hangs in the background, noticed by a few but ignored by most.

But there was more to it than that, a part of himself he'd never been able to understand or control—an almost pathological need to keep essential pieces of himself hidden away, even from the woman he loved. It wasn't a matter of privacy, or a safety mechanism, or fear of revealing too much or too little of himself. It wasn't anything that he could define. A genetic quirk, a birth defect. Bad wiring. Every time he tried to put meaningful thoughts or feelings into words, it was as if his brain short-circuited and rendered him mute.

He knew this was what had laid the foundation for the wall between Shelby and him. His inability to give her children, the business failure, the job loss six months ago, the days spent apart because of the demands of her EMT job—they were just bricks stacked on top of the foundation. You can't hide from the person you live with, much less from yourself, and expect a relationship to roll smoothly along and outlast the succession of crises that had plagued theirs.

Well, he wouldn't be hiding this latest load of bricks much longer. Four days from now, five at the most, he'd gird himself and dump it all over her because he had no other choice.

The rain seemed to be letting up a little, though the cloud ceiling was low and gouts of heavy mist rolled in from the ocean close by on their left. A road sign ahead indicated a series of sharp descending turns that shouldn't be taken at more than twenty-five. He was into the second switchback when he saw the sweep of oncoming headlights. The other driver was going too fast for the conditions, crowding the center of the highway, his headlights on high bright. Shelby jerked erect, bracing herself against the dash, as Macklin swung the wheel hard right. The other driver also corrected in time; the car hissed past them with not much room to spare.

Macklin said, "Christ, that was close."

"Too close."

"Damn idiot. Cops all over the road tonight, but none around when you need one."

"Must be a lot of accidents on this highway, especially in weather like this. I wonder what kind of EMT service they have up here."

"Let's hope we don't find out."

Shelby resettled herself. "How much farther?"

They were coming out of the last switchback, onto a stretch that hooked around a deep inlet bordered on the north by a high, sheer cliff. Strong waves lashed at the base of the cliff, sending up huge jets and fans of spray. Here and there along the cliff top and the wooded ridge above it, lights glowed mistily.

"Not far now," he said. "That should be Seacrest up there."

It was. Grocery store, café, antique and crafts store, combination gas station, garage, and towing service—all closed, even though it wasn't yet seven o'clock. Small inn down in a hollow and a short row of bed-and-breakfasts on one side of the highway, none of which was doing much if any business. Ben had told him Seacrest had once been a thriving lumber town, one of the larger doghole ports along the coast where milled timber was loaded onto steamers bound south to San Francisco, north to Seattle. You wouldn't know it from the way it looked now—

"Speak of the devil," Shelby said.

"What?"

"Parking lot next to the grocery."

Macklin saw it then—a county sheriff's cruiser, dark, parked just outside the building's shadow. "Watching for speeders, probably. Why the hell didn't he nab that asshole down below?"

"The asshole probably wasn't speeding when he came through here."

They were out of the village as quickly as they'd come into it, dropping down again past a scatter of private homes. After that the dark thread of the highway ran through stands of trees, past open spaces spotted with clumps of gorse and pampas grass on the seaward side.

Another half mile, and the rain came pounding down again. Macklin slowed to thirty, hunching forward, looking for the first of Ben's landmarks—an old and thickly overgrown country cemetery. Pretty soon it came up on the left and he checked the odometer: 2.1 miles to go. The highway cut inland past the cemetery, then back up toward the sea until it was running along the rim of a section of barren cliffs. Guardrails indicated a long drop to the rough seas below.

Second landmark: a meadow bisected by a eucalyptus-lined driveway leading to a group of ranch buildings. Six-tenths of a mile from there. The highway curved inland again, then back to where dense woods replaced the open space along the cliff tops. Almost there. He began looking for the signpost that would read Tobias Creek Road. The next bluffside turn beyond Tobias Creek was Ocean Point Lane, where Ben's cottage was located.

The signpost should have been easy to spot, but it wasn't. In the darkness and downpour, he missed it.

He knew he had when the odometer clicked off an extra tenth of a mile. He asked Shelby if she'd seen the Tobias Creek sign.

"No. Gone too far?"

"I think so. Better find a place to turn around."

Another tenth of a mile before he found one where he could make the turn safely, then two-tenths of a mile back to the south. The Prius's head lights picked out a handful of turnings both left and right, but no signpost.

"Shit," he said. "Where is it?"

"Don't tell me we're lost."

"We're not lost. It's just that I don't see Tobias Creek Road."

"Maybe we haven't come to it yet."

"It's supposed to be right along here."

"Maybe the odometer is off."

"No. All the other landmarks checked."

Macklin turned into the nearest side road, but it was unmarked and barred by a gate. He backed out and made another slow pass along the highway. Still no sign for Tobias Creek Road. Or for Ocean Point Lane.

Shelby said, "We can't keep driving around all night looking."

"There must be houses around here, somebody to ask . . ."

"You see any lights? I don't."

"Dammit, I wish we had GPS."

"Well, we don't." She was quiet for a few seconds, then she chuckled in a wry way. "Maybe there *is* one around when we need one."

"What?"

"A cop. The sheriff's deputy parked in Seacrest. He ought to know where Tobias Creek Road and Ocean Point Lane are."

"It's three miles back to Seacrest. And he might have moved by now."

"If he's not there, we'll ask directions at one of the B&Bs. Unless you have a better suggestion." Her voice had an edge that said she was running out of patience.

He said, "No, no better suggestion. Back to Seacrest."

Only three miles, but it seemed a lot longer than five minutes before the village lights appeared. He slowed to a crawl as he passed the row of B&Bs. Ahead the night-lights and scattered Christmas decorations swam up blurrily through the rain.

"He's still there," Shelby said.

When Macklin made the turn into the grocery parking lot, the Prius's headlights flicked over the darkened patrol car and briefly picked out a man-shape behind the steering wheel. He eased to stop alongside, started to roll down his window. The reaction to that surprised him. Instead of following suit, the deputy fired up his engine and jumped the cruiser ahead and around behind them at an angle. Then it stopped again, blocking the exit, its lights still off.

"What's he doing?"

Macklin shook his head, looking into the rearview mirror. Nothing happened for fifteen seconds or so. Then the cruiser's door popped open and the deputy came out, moving quickly away from the vehicle until he was ten yards to Macklin's side of the Prius. He stopped there, standing in a slight, stiff crouch, one tail of his black rain slicker swept back and his hand on his holstered weapon. The other hand held a six-cell flashlight, which he raised and waggled in a commanding, get-out-of-the-car gesture.

Macklin hesitated. They'd brought an umbrella, but it was somewhere among the cartons and luggage in the backseat. The hell with it; the deputy was still gesturing. He got out, pulling his coat collar up tight under his chin.

Immediately the flashlight beam stabbed out and pinned him. He blinked against the light, the icy bite of wind and rain in his face; lifted an arm to shield his eyes. The beam held on him for a few seconds before it lowered. The deputy shortened the distance between them to five feet, the lower halves of his slicker billowing around him like half-folded wings. Under the brim of an oilskin-covered cap, his face was young, pale-featured, tightly drawn. A thick mustache bristled on his upper lip.

Bewildered, Macklin said, "Anything wrong, officer?" He had to almost shout to make himself heard above the scree of the wind.

The deputy moved again without answering, past him and close to the Prius. He shined the flash through the driver's window. Shelby's white face appeared, then disappeared as the light flicked off. The deputy seemed to relax a little as he turned toward Macklin, but when he spoke, his voice was curt and officious.

"Something I can do for you folks?"

"We're staying at a friend's cottage three miles north of here, but we can't seem to find it."

"So that's why you came back. I saw you pass through a while ago."

"That's why. We thought maybe you could help."

"Never been to this cottage before?"

"No. First time."

"What's your friend's name?"

"Ben Coulter. He lives in Los Altos Hills—the cottage is his vacation place."

"Not the usual time of year for a vacation, weather being what it is."

"This week is the only time my wife could get off from her job."

"Uh-huh. Your name?"

"Jay Macklin."

"From?"

"Cupertino."

"Let's have a look at your driver's license, Mr. Macklin."

"Out here in the rain?"

"Unless you have some objection."

"No, no objection."

Under a pair of watchful eyes, Macklin slipped the license out of his wallet and handed it over. The deputy backed up with it, as if to establish a safe distance, and peered at it in the ray from his six-cell. The way he studied it, for nearly half a minute, told Macklin he was committing the information to memory.

The light flicked off and the deputy moved closer again to return the license. He said as Macklin put it back into his wallet, "Where'd you say your friend's cottage is located?"

"Three miles north. One of three homes on Ocean Point Lane. The turnoff is just past Tobias Creek Road, but I couldn't find a signpost for either one."

"That's because they're gone. Stolen just before Christmas—kids, probably. The county hasn't had time to replace them."

"Can you tell us how to get there?"

"Do better than that. I know Ocean Point Lane—I'll lead you there. Which of the properties is your friend's?"

"The middle one."

The deputy nodded, as if he'd gotten the right answer to a quiz question. "All right. Better get back inside before you get any wetter."

"Thanks, officer. It's a hell of a night."

"That's right, Mr. Macklin. A hell of a night."

He was dripping wet, his hair plastered to his head, when he slid under the wheel. Shelby had dredged up the blanket they kept in the back; she handed it to him, partly unfolded.

"What was that all about?"

"I don't have a clue," Macklin said, wiping his face. "He was uptight about something, suspicious."

"Having to work on a night like this, probably."

"It was more than that."

"On the lookout for somebody driving a car like ours, then."

"Maybe. But the way he acted . . . I don't know. It just didn't seem like normal behavior for a sheriff's deputy."

"Who knows what's normal up here. Did you get directions?"

"He knows where Ben's cottage is. He's going to lead us there."

"Good. Then we won't miss it again."

The patrol car's lights were on now, its engine idling—the deputy waiting for them. Macklin put the Prius in gear, looped around slowly to follow the cruiser out onto the deserted highway. Everything was okay now, the long drive almost over, but he couldn't help the feeling that something about the deputy's behavior wasn't quite right. And for no reason that he could understand.

TWO

OCEAN POINT LANE WAS a narrow blacktop, its intersection with Highway 1 screened by timber on both sides. No mailboxes, which meant all three properties were second homes where the owners didn't receive mail. Even if there'd been signposts, Ocean Point was all but invisible in the squalling darkness and Jay might have missed it anyway.

The lane curled in through dense woods that crowded close on both sides. The patrol car's and the Prius's headlights, moving in tandem, were like miners' helmet lamps boring into a dank, stalactitic cave. The image lingered in Shelby's mind, put a spot of cold between her shoulder blades. There was very little that she was afraid of; nurse's training and ten years as an EMT had thickened her skin and toughened her defenses to the point where she could view all sorts of human suffering with professional detachment. But she'd never quite lost her fear of the dark.

She'd had it as far back as she could remember. Not of ordinary darkness, the light-tinged kind where you had some limited vision of objects or shapes. Of blackness so complete you couldn't see anything at all, the kind a blind person must feel—she couldn't imagine anything more terrible than losing her sight. Being alone in a place without light was like being trapped and slowly suffocating in an airless void. She'd made the mistake of saying this to her mother once, when she was little. Mom, the no-nonsense disciplinarian who didn't believe in indulging "the silly notions of children," who'd sought to "cure" the fear by forcing

Shelby to sleep without a night-light and punishing her if she was caught doing otherwise, like the time she'd burrowed under the covers with a smuggled-in flashlight that Mom had found still burning in the morning. The fear hadn't evolved into a consuming or crippling adult phobia; she had it under control. But empty, lightless places like these woods still had the power to scrape at her nerves, tighten her sphincter.

She wanted to be here even less now. *Why* had she let Jay talk her into this trip? Well, yes, because he seemed to want it so badly; he didn't ask her for much and agreeing had seemed like granting a favor as well as taking the path of least resistance. Miserable year for him, for both of them; and the marriage was rocky enough without making it worse by fighting him on a relatively minor issue. She had her bad points, God knew, but selfishness wasn't one of them.

Still, what was the point? Did he think four days and nights on this isolated section of the Mendocino coast would somehow bring them closer together, magically lead to a solution of their problems? If anything, the enforced proximity might just make things worse. She'd almost rather spend New Year's Eve on the ambulance, dealing with all the carnage that ringing out the old, ringing in the new always brought. Or spend it with Douglas—

No.

She wasn't going to think about Douglas. Not now.

The blacktop curved off to the left to skirt a long, high wooden fence—the first of the three properties. They passed a driveway barred by a pair of closed gates. Large parcel of land, whatever buildings that were on it hidden by more wind-whipped trees. Somebody's summer estate. Dreary and lifeless in the driving rain.

A couple of hundred yards beyond where the fence ended, the woods thinned and Ben Coulter's property appeared. His parcel was much smaller, the cottage built closer to the road and nearer the bluff's edge because of an inland bend in the shoreline. The upper half of the cottage, squarish, sided by a brick chimney that extended above the roofline, was visible behind a wood-stake fence two feet lower than the estate's. A covered carport stood just off the lane on the far side. The deputy slowed and pulled onto the verge beyond the carport, to give Jay room to turn in off the lane.

He said, "Finally," and switched off engine and lights.

Shelby didn't respond. Through more trees to the north she could make out a faint light shimmer. Security lights on the third property, she thought. Either that, or some other misguided souls were spending what remained of the holidays here. The sense of isolation might not be so bad if there were other people around for at least part of their stay.

"Deputy's still sitting there," Jay said. "What's he waiting for?"

"Us to go inside, probably."

"Why?"

"To make sure we belong here."

"Christ. Why would he think I lied to him?"

Edgy Jay. Worrywart Jay. He hadn't always been like that. He'd had self-assurance, self-esteem when she met him; he'd been grounded and motivated their first few years together, before all the misfortune began to wear him down. Qualities that had made it easy for her to fall in love with him. She'd believed then that he was the first important person in her life she wouldn't end up having to take care of. Not that she blamed him that it had turned out otherwise; none of the bad luck was his fault. But his moodiness, his defeatest attitude, his increasing dependency, put a strain on her tolerance.

"Why don't you go ask him?" she said.

"Oh, sure, and make him even more suspicious."

"All right, then. Let's go on in."

On the way from the carport to a locked gate in the fence, she pulled the hood of her coat over her head. The cold rain seemed to stream inside anyway, stinging against her face, chilling her after the warmth of the car. Jay fumbled with the key Ben had given him, got the gate open. A short walkway opened into a kind of patio floored with wooden squares, like a patterned inlay, black now from the rain and strewn with small pine boughs and needles torn loose and deposited by the wind. Beyond the patio an area of open ground sloped downward, flanked by bent and swaying pines. Above the wind's shriek she could hear the boom of surf, but the ocean was invisible behind a shroud of misty blackness.

They hurried across the patio, up a few steps to a low, open deck that stretched around the side and probably extended the full oceanfront width of the cottage. Jay did some more fumbling with the door key—"My fingers are numb"—and when he finally got the lock to turn, she all but pushed him inside.

A damp, musty smell dilated her nostrils. How long since Ben Coulter and his family had been up here? Last summer sometime?

The interior jumped into pale focus: Jay had found the light switch.

Shelby looked around, expecting the worst but not finding it. The cottage had been built in the early seventies, Ben had told Jay, but the furnishings and decor were neither old nor shabby-chic. The living room was good-sized, the fireplace at the opposite end with a comfortable-looking leather sofa and a couple of chairs grouped in front of it. The beige rug on the floor looked new. There were several oddly shaped pieces of driftwood on the fireplace mantel and seascapes on two walls, but mercifully, none of the tacky stuff like fishnets and fake glass floats and whale lamps and dolphin sculptures that infested so many seaside homes. Two big recliners were arranged in front of a pair of windows facing the sea; blinds covered the windows now, but she could hear the harsh beat of rain against glass.

"Nice, Shel, don't you think?"

"Very homey. Rustic as hell." He gave her one of his hurt-puppy looks. Heart melters, she called them, and they still had the capacity to soften her. "Sorry. I didn't mean to sound bitchy. It is a nice place."

"I'll start getting things out of the car. You stay here where it's dry." A blast of cold swirled into the room as he went out.

Next to the fireplace was a wood box filled with newspaper, kindling, and cut logs. Let Jay make a fire, she thought. It would probably wound what was left of his ego if she did it. There had to be some other source of heat . . . yes, a baseboard heater that stretched along the front wall under the blind-covered windows. She found the controls, turned the heat up as high as it would go.

A small kitchen and dining area opened off the living room, separated from it by a breakfast bar. Beyond, a short hallway led to bedrooms and bathrooms. Two bedrooms, one and a half baths.

The front door blew open again, literally, letting in another blast of wind and rain. Jay struggled through with two cartons of the food and liquor they'd brought with them, shouldered the door shut behind him. He was panting a little, as if he'd been carrying a heavy load uphill. Out of shape. He hadn't gone running with her in more than a year, and he'd given up going to the gym to work out because the membership cost too much. He still walked a couple of miles every day, or said he did, and watched his carb intake and his cholesterol, but—

"He was still there when I went out."

"Who? The deputy?"

"He backed in next to the car while I was getting this stuff." Jay set the cartons on the breakfast bar. "Rolled down his window and stuck his head out. You know what he said?"

"How could I? I wasn't there."

"He said, 'You folks be careful while you're here.' What do you suppose he meant by that?"

"He probably didn't mean anything by it. Just one of those things law enforcement people say."

"No. He made it sound like a warning."

Trying her patience again. Sometimes Jay made her feel the way Mom had, more like a nursemaid than a loved one. "Is he gone now?"

"Yeah, he's gone."

"Then will you please stop obsessing about him? We'll never see the man again."

Jay went back out to fetch their suitcases. While he was gone, Shelby unpacked the cartons. The refrigerator was plugged in, so no problem there; there was even a little ice in trays in the freezer compartment. She put the perishables inside, left the bottles of Beefeater and vermouth and the jar of olives on the counter. A double martini in front of a hot fire ought to make her warm again.

The master bedroom was small, the bed a standard double that meant they'd be sleeping close together. He would probably want sex at some point and she supposed she'd accommodate him. He'd always been an accomplished and considerate lover, with as much concern for her plea-sure as his own, and in the beginning their lovemaking had been fueled by passion and experimentation; but it had slacked off gradually through all the problems and setbacks, until now it was infrequent and mostly mechanical and no longer satisfying, at least for her.

He never complained, said every time how good it was, but then so did she. Pretense. For him, too, maybe. How could she know? He wouldn't talk about things that mattered to him; wouldn't tell her anything about the recurring and obviously terrifying nightmare that plagued his sleep; wouldn't confide in her or allow her more than brief glimpses of what was going on inside his head. She'd tried dozens of times over the years, especially during the crisis periods—when he'd lost the restaurant, when he'd been laid off from Conray Foods—and never once had she gotten a satisfactory response. Closed off. And by degrees closing her off, too, until now they were more like cohabiting roommates than husband and wife.

She unpacked the suitcases while he rubbed down and put on dry clothes. There were martini glasses in one of the kitchen cupboards; she put two in the freezer to chill. Then she mixed a batch of martinis, as she usually did because she made them better than Jay; he tended to use too much vermouth.

It was warmer in the cottage now, but not warm enough for her to shed her down jacket yet. The damp, musty smell was still pervasive. Wind howled in the chimney, chill breaths of it stirring ashes inside the fireplace. Four days. There was a TV and a combination VCR and DVD player, but no cable; a small collection of DVDs and VHS tapes were all you could watch. There was also a radio/CD boom box, the kind with Civil Defense and police bands, some music CDs of various types, and a shelf of paper-backs, mostly the historical romances that Kate considered steamy and she found overblown and silly. Four days. Pretense and superficial conversation and unsatisfying sex. If it stormed the whole time they were here, she'd be diving into the gin a lot earlier than seven P.M. by New Year's Eve.

Jay came back out as she was pouring a martini for herself. He said, "None for me."

"I thought you'd like one after that interminable drive."

"Just a glass of wine. That's all I want."

New development, this. Jay liked martinis as much as she did; cocktails together when she wasn't working the night shift had been one of their more pleasurable rituals. But lately he'd quit drinking hard liquor, cut back on wine as well. All he'd said when she asked him about it was that he'd been drinking too much and felt it was a good idea to ease off. Subtle dig at her? Probably not; he hadn't suggested she cut back herself. Still, the holiday season was a funny time to make a decision usually reserved for the New Year.

Wind and hard rain slammed against the cottage, rattling the windows and the door in its frame, as he poured a small glass of wine for himself. He said then, "I'll make a fire. You just enjoy your drink."

Enjoy it? She swallowed half of the martini, felt its warmth spreading through her. Better. But she still didn't take off her jacket.

From one end of the sofa she watched Jay arranging kindling and crumpled newspaper on the hearth. Man, the firemaker. Once he'd been robust, his dark hair thick and curly, his color high and his body radiating strength. An athlete in high school and his first two years of college, especially good at baseball—a power-hitting centerfielder who might have gotten a pro contract if he hadn't damaged his knee in a home-plate collision in his sophomore year at UC Santa Cruz. Now . . . fifteen pounds lighter, hair thinning and losing its luster, shoulders tending to draw down instead of up and back when he moved. There were times, watching him like this, when she barely recognized the Jay Macklin she'd married twelve years ago, as if that man had somehow morphed into a near stranger.

The fantasy came over her again, as it did now and then at odd moments. She imagined that the familiar lines and angles of him were shrinking, blurring, losing definition; that he was dematerializing a little more each day, becoming harder to see clearly; that eventually he would turn fuzzily transparent, like a ghost, so you'd be able to see daylight through him, and then finally he would disappear altogether—the new invisible man.

She couldn't bear to witness something like that, the literal slipping down and fading away of the man she'd once loved . . . no, still loved, or she wouldn't still be with him. If that was what was going to happen, she'd be gone before the deterioration was complete.

Maybe gone sooner than that, she thought.

In spite of herself, a comparison image of Douglas flashed into her mind. Strong, solid. Not particularly good-looking, but those intense and frank hazel eyes were more appealing than any pretty-boy features. Another image: the seemingly effortless way he went about his duties in South Bay General's ER—capable, commanding, in complete control no matter what the emergency or crisis case. Another: the openness of his smile when he spoke to her, so that she felt he was not only an honest man but one who seldom if ever hid his true feelings . . .

Shelby shook herself, hard, to rid her mind of the images and the thoughts that went with them. Emptied her glass in one stinging gulp.

Jay was on his feet now, poking among the pieces of driftwood on the mantel. "There aren't any matches here," he said.

"I'll look in the kitchen." She wanted another martini anyway.

She opened drawers and cabinets. The Coulters kept the cottage well stocked: liquor, coffee, spices, condiments. But no matches.

A door next to the stove opened onto a cramped utility porch. Washer and dryer. Microwave. Full wine rack. Vacuum cleaner. Pantry filled with canned and packaged goods and cleaning supplies—and nothing else.

She went back into the kitchen. Jay was at a catchall closet next to the breakfast bar, rummaging among the shelves. "Find any, Shel?"

"No."

"Don't seem to be any in here, either."

"Maybe in one of the bedrooms."

She went to look. Nothing.

Jay was still at the closet when she came back. He said, "Well, hell," when he saw that she was empty-handed.

"You sure there're no matches in there?" she asked.

"Look for yourself."

The closet shelves were packed with all sorts of odds and ends. A pocket-size portable radio, flashlight, batteries, candles, hand tools, local phone directories, napkins and placemats, decks of playing cards, even Scrabble and backgammon games. Everything you might want or need except the one essential you were looking for.

"Ben must not have realized he was out or he'd have mentioned it."

"Good old Ben."

"Well, it's not a crisis. We'll buy some in Seacrest tomorrow. I'll just use the stove tonight."

"It's electric."

"Doesn't matter. I can light a twist of newspaper on one of the burners, use that to start the fire."

"Just don't light up anything else on the way."

He fetched a couple of sheets of newspaper, rolled them up as he moved into the kitchen to turn on the stove burner.

Shelby picked up the martini pitcher, started to pour her glass full again.

And all the lights went out.

THREE

MACKLIN STOOD BLINKING IN the sudden blackness. He heard Shelby suck in her breath, the clatter of the pitcher as she set it down hard on the countertop. "Shel? You okay?"

"Don't worry, I'm not going to panic."

"Power'll probably come right back on."

She didn't say anything.

He groped his way around the wet bar, saying, "There's a flashlight in the closet there—"

"I know, I saw it. The batteries better be good."

She moved away from him, sideways to the closet. With the lights off, the furious whistling, rattling sounds of the storm seemed magnified. A power outage . . . just what they didn't need right now.

A blade of light slashed through the dark, carving out whitish jigsaw pieces as Shelby swung it up and around toward him. "We'd better go sit down," she said.

He followed her across the living room to the couch. She laid the flashlight on an end table and left it burning, so that the beam made a stationary white circle on the fireplace bricks. He knew she'd had a small scare. She was a borderline nyctophobe; had insisted on sleeping with a night-light on the entire time they'd been married. He suspected that one of the reasons she'd become an EMT was that it was a job requiring a certain amount of night work—her way of battling the demon.

They sat listening to the wind and rain, waiting. Minutes ticked away—five, ten. He wanted to say something, couldn't think of anything that she'd want to hear. He settled for putting a hand on her leg, giving it a gentle squeeze; the muscles and tendons were taut. Shelby's gaze remained fixed on the white circle.

The silence thickened between them until he couldn't stand it any longer. "You get occasional power failures in remote areas like this," he said. "But they don't usually last very long."

"Unless the storm knocks down power lines."

He had no answer for that.

"It's cold in here again," she said. "Another hour and it'll be like a meat locker."

"There's always bed, blankets, and body heat."

No answer from her this time.

"What do you want to do then? Drive back to Seacrest, take a room in one of those B&Bs?"

"The power'll be out there too. If we had matches for a fire, candles—" She broke off and then said, "Maybe we can borrow some."

"Where? Seacrest?"

"The neighbors to the north. I'm pretty sure I saw lights through the trees when we arrived."

"Probably security lights."

"We can go find out, can't we? It's better than sitting here freezing. If nobody's home, we'll drive into the village."

In the bedroom they each held the torch while the other put on rain gear. Outside, Jay lighted their run to the carport. The storm created wildly gyrating shapes of the pines to the north, but just before he clambered in behind the Prius's wheel he saw the shimmers of light in that direction.

The narrow lane was carpeted with pine needles and wind-torn branches, one of the branches large enough that Macklin had to ease out around it at a crawl. The stand of trees that separated Ben's property from the one on this side was a couple of hundred yards in length; after two-thirds of that distance, it thinned out and ended at a high fence that extended out to the bluff's edge and continued parallel to the road. Above the fence he could see the upper part of the house, portions of tall dark windows and angled roofline; the pale haze of light came from below. Wood smoke bellowed out of a stone chimney and was immediately shredded and whipped away by the swirling wind.

Shelby said, "Definitely somebody home."

"They must have an auxiliary generator. That's the only way they can have power when we don't."

The blacktop dead-ended at the base of a rocky headland that rose at the property's far perimeter. There was a double gate in the fence, one half closed and the other half open. Drive right in? Might as well. Let the the headlights tell the people here right away that they had visitors.

He made the turn through the gate. The front of the house was dark; the light came through windows at the sides and back. Big place, modernistic in design, built of redwood and glass halfway to the bluff's edge and partially in the shadow of the headland. Three cars sat on a parking area a short distance inside the gate: a medium-size SUV, a four-door sedan, and a low-slung sports car. Macklin pulled up next to the sports job—Porsche Boxster, looked like, a make and model he'd always coveted—and shut off the headlamps.

"Want to wait here?"

"No," Shelby said. "I'll go with you."

The front door stayed closed as they hurried along a short flagstone path onto a porch shielded by a slanted overhang and palely lit by a recessed spot. Macklin found the doorbell, pushed it. A minute passed; no response. But he sensed somebody on the other side watching them through a peephole in the door. He blew on his cold hands, rang the bell again. And still the door didn't open.

"Leery of strangers showing up on a night like this," he said against Shelby's ear. "Maybe I should—"

"Who're you?" Man's voice from inside, loud and unfriendly. "What do you want?"

"Sorry to disturb you," Macklin called out. "We're friends of Ben Coulter, staying at his cottage down the way. Just arrived before the power went out."

"I asked you what you want."

"Can you let us have some matches? We didn't bring any and there're none in the cottage."

Silence. Then, "Matches, for Christ's sake," barely audible in a lull in the storm-throb, directed to a second person behind the door who answered in a voice too low for the words to be distinguishable. But Macklin thought it belonged to a woman.

Shelby pressed up against him, taking hold of his arm, either because she was cold or in an effort to gain sympathy from the peephole watcher. She called out, "It's freezing in the cottage. We'd really appreciate the help."

The woman's voice said, clearly this time, "Oh, for heaven's sake, just let them come in."

"No."

"Yes."

A chain rattled and the door opened to reveal a slender young blonde woman dressed in slacks and a bulky knit sweater. Behind her, a big, blocky-faced man in his early forties said, "You always get what you want, don't you, Claire?" The woman didn't answer. When she widened the door opening, the man backed off a few paces and stood scowling. Macklin had a glimpse then of two other people in a broad sunken living room beyond a short foyer—a lean, sandy-haired male standing by the steps and a dark-haired female on a couch in front of a massive curving fireplace, both with glasses in their hands.

The blonde woman said, "Come in, I'm sorry you had to stand out there so long." Her tone and her smile seemed almost eager, as if she were welcoming acquaintances rather than strangers.

Shelby went in first, Macklin behind her, and then she stopped abruptly. He saw why a couple of seconds later, when he had his first clear look at the big man.

There was a gun in his hand.

It wasn't pointed at them; he was holding it muzzle down along his right leg. A large automatic on a squarish aluminum or polymer frame.

"It's all right, don't worry," the blonde woman said, and shut the door against the bitter night. Then, to the man, "Brian, please—put that thing away. These people are no threat."

"I don't like to take chances."

"He thinks he's back on military guardhouse duty," the sandy-haired man said. "Or Clint Eastwood in *Dirty Harry.*"

The woman on the couch said, "Why shouldn't he be careful? We're all a little spooked."

"I'm not," the blocky-faced man said flatly. As if to prove it, he opened a closet door and made the automatic disappear inside.

The blonde woman looked relieved. "I'm Claire Lomax. This is my husband, Brian. And these are the Deckers—Brian's sister, Paula, and her husband, Gene."

"Jay Macklin. My wife, Shelby."

"Shelby Hunter," she said.

Again, as always. If he neglected to add her last name in an introduction, she did it herself, immediately and automatically. And as always, it saddened him a little. Not because she'd chosen to keep her birth name—that had never bothered him—but because of what her making an issue of it subtly implied. Separate identities, linked by marriage but with a gap between them that could never be bridged.

"Shelby," Claire Lomax said, "that's an unusual name."

"It was my maternal grandmother's."

"Mmm. Well, you must be chilled. Come in, sit by the fire, have something to drink before you go."

"We don't want to intrude—"

"You're not intruding. Are they, Brian?"

Lomax said nothing. He was still scowling.

Macklin was about to decline the invitation. Seeing Lomax with that automatic had made him edgy again. There was something else, too, a kind of charged atmosphere—as if there were frictions among the four of them and he and Shelby had interrupted a tense interaction.

But Shelby didn't seem to feel it; she surprised him by saying, "We'd like to, if you're sure you don't mind. I haven't been warm since the power went out."

"I know what you mean," Claire said, "it's a miserable night. Here, let me take your coats."

"Sure, come and join us," the dark-haired woman said. "Misery loves company."

Her husband said, "Shut up, Paula," without looking at her.

"Fuck you."

Gene Decker laughed as if she'd said something funny, but the glare he directed at her was venomous. He tilted his glass, drained it in a long swallow. "I can use another drink myself."

"So can I. God, yes."

"You've had your quota, honeybunch."

"Like hell I have. If you won't make me another one, Brian will."

Lomax didn't move.

Tension here, all right. You could feel it, almost hear it—a subaural crackling like echoes from the pitch-pine logs burning in the fireplace. Whatever was going on with these people, Macklin didn't want any part of it. But Shelby had committed them; he couldn't just drag her out of here. Couldn't have managed a quick exit anyhow because she'd already shrugged out of her coat. Nothing he could do then but shed his own coat, then follow her down the three steps into the living room.

Paula made room for them on the couch. She was about Shelby's age, plump and top-heavy, her round cheeks irregularly flushed like a person afflicted with rosacea. When Claire asked what they'd like to drink, Shelby said she'd been having a martini before the lights went out. At ease as usual in a social situation, even among bad-mannered, boozy strangers like these.

Decker said, "Martinis are my speciality," and crossed to a built-in, stone-fronted bar. "Gin or vodka? Up or on the rocks?"

"Gin, please. Up."

"Same for you, Macklin?"

"No. Nothing for me, thanks."

"Oh, come on. Free booze is free booze."

"Just not thirsty."

"Okay, then. More for the rest of us."

Lomax was still standing in the foyer. An imposing figure, a couple of inches over six feet and wide through the shoulders and neck, dressed casually like the others in slacks and sweater. His bristly rust-colored hair was cut so short his scalp gleamed pink and shiny through it. He'd lost his scowl; now his beard-dark face was set in tight, unreadable lines.

His wife sat down in a chair on Shelby's right. She was at least fifteen years younger than Lomax, Macklin thought. Eyes the striking color of smoked pearl, luminous with some veiled emotion . . . anxiety? High cheekbones, pale skin a little liquor-reddened, long, slender throat, a model's slim figure. But her beauty was the fragile kind that would fade or turn gaunt with age, and marred by lines around her mouth and faint shadows under her eyes. Shelby was just the opposite, he thought, more attractive now than when he'd married her; the strength and character in her face were lacking in Claire Lomax's.

"So, then," she said. "Where are you folks from?"

Macklin told them.

"And you're friends of the Coulters?"

"Ben and I went to college together—UC Santa Cruz."

"We've met him and his wife—Kate, isn't it?—but we don't know them well."

"Kate, yes."

"How long are you staying? Through New Year's?"

"Until New Year's Day."

"Good! So are we. We'll have to get together again, maybe on New Year's Eve." She seemed to need to talk, as if she were afraid of dead air; her words came quickly, a little breathlessly. Macklin wondered if she was drunk. There wasn't any doubt that Paula was. Decker, too, if less obviously. "All of us live in Santa Rosa. We've been here since Christmas Eve. We thought it'd be fun to spend the holidays here this year, now that the house is finished."

"Some fun," Paula said. "Wackos on the loose inside and out."

"The only wacko in here is you," Decker said from the bar.

"Hurry up with those drinks, will you?"

"Can't rush perfection. Santa will deliver."

"Santa. Jesus."

"Ho, ho, ho."

Claire ignored them. "Brian's an architect. He designed this house, everything exactly the way he wanted it. Isn't that fireplace wonderful?"

It was, and Macklin said so. Built of native stone, it transcribed a long, graceful curve outward from the side wall, with the hearth in the middle of the curve and open to this room and the one on the other side, probably the kitchen. The bedrooms would be along a front hallway that led off the foyer. The rest of the living room was as impressive as the fireplace, if a little too colorless for his taste. Heavy redwood ceiling beams, dark wood paneling, floors partially covered by black-and-white woven rugs. A four-foot-square painting on one wall, of a stormy, cloud-ridden sky at sunset, added a moody note. Something brighter, with primary colors, would've been better. So would a Christmas tree, a wreath, some kind of holiday decoration, but there were none visible anywhere.

Lomax finally made up his mind to join them, but he didn't sit down. He stood at a distance, like an overseer. "The house isn't finished yet," he said.

"Well, it is, but Brian means little things, little touches he's not satisfied with—"

"I don't like that, Claire. You know I don't."

"What don't you like?"

"You speaking for me. Why do you keep doing it?"

"Well, I'm sorry, I didn't mean . . . Oh, good, the drinks."

Decker was there with a tray. Martini in a broad-rimmed glass with a lemon peel instead of olives, four mixed drinks that from their color were probably Scotch and water. He handed them out, the palest of the three to his wife, who glared at him but didn't say anything. Lomax refused the last glass with a curt, "No, I've had enough for tonight."

"Another party pooper."

"Why don't you drink what you sell, instead of swilling Scotch all the time?"

"Ah, yes, fine California wine. How does that Omar quote go? 'I wonder what the vintners guzzle one half so precious as the stuff they sell'?"

"Guzzle. Very funny."

"Gene is a sales rep for Eagle Mountain Winery," Claire said. "In the Russian River valley."

Paula made a derisive noise. "They work him like a dog too—or I should say like a son of a bitch. Would you believe even on Christmas Day, so I had to drive up here by myself?"

Decker said, "Here we go again."

"What was it you were working on this time, sweetie—blonde, brunette, or redhead?"

"Why don't you finish your drink and pass out?"

"Fuck you."

Decker didn't laugh this time. "Isn't she a treasure? Too bad she's not the buried kind."

There was an awkward moment before Claire asked Macklin, "What do you do, Jay? For a living, I mean?"

"I'm between jobs right now."

"Another victim of the goddamn economy," Decker said. "What profession did you get tossed out of?"

"I've done a lot of things," he said evasively, and couldn't think of anything to add that didn't sound lame or self-defensive.

Shelby rescued him. "Jay's passion is owning a quality restaurant. We did own one, as a matter of fact, for three years in Morgan Hill. Macklin's Grotto. Seafood specialties."

"What happened?"

"The same thing that happens to a lot of good restaurants these days. Too much expense and not enough customers."

Talking about the restaurant—thinking about it—was still painful. To change the subject Macklin said, "Shelby's the breadwinner now. She's an EMT."

"You mean a paramedic?" Claire said. "Oh, that's interesting. I know there are women who do that work, but I've never met one. It must be rewarding to help people who . . . people in trouble."

"Yes," Shelby said.

"But stressful, too. Do you work long hours?"

"Sometimes. Nights as well as days."

"Must play hell with your love life," Decker said.

Another brief, awkward silence. Paula broke it by saying, "What's it like to *have* a love life? Been so long, I've forgotten."

"If you weren't an ice maiden, maybe you'd find out."

"Damn you, Gene! That's a lie and you know it."

Lomax said angrily, "You two make me sick." Knots of muscle bulged on the twin points of his jawline. He stalked across to the fireplace, keeping his back turned to the rest of them; pitched another log atop the burning stack, then used a poker to jab it into place.

Macklin had had enough. "I think we'd better be going." He looked at Shelby as he said it, hoping she wouldn't offer any argument. She didn't; she sat silently looking into her almost empty glass.

"Oh, no, please," Claire said, "don't leave yet."

"We need to unpack, get settled."

"It's only eight thirty. We haven't eaten yet—you're welcome to stay for dinner. Aren't they, Brian?"

"No," Lomax said.

"Brian . . ."

"I said no." He jabbed harder at the fire, sending up sparks and glowing embers. "No means no this time."

Macklin said quickly, "We couldn't stay anyway. We . . . brought a casserole from home."

"But you can't cook it with the power out."

"It's the kind you can eat cold."

Lomax lowered the poker, clattered it into its holder. His squarish face still showed anger when he turned. "They're ready to leave, Claire. Go get the matches they asked for."

"The master has spoken," Decker said. "Always obey the master."

Claire snapped at him, "Gene, *please*. Do you always have to be such a wise-ass?"

"You bet he does," Paula said. "It's the only other thing he's good at besides infidelity."

"You're as bad as he is. For God's sake."

They were all on their feet now. Claire fetched a box of long safety matches from a wood box on the hearth. Macklin said he'd replace them tomorrow, she said that wasn't necessary. Into the vestibule then, into his and Shelby's coats. Pleasure to meet you all, thanks for the matches and the drinks, hope to see you again. Claire shook hands with them; none of the other three bothered. And finally he and Shelby were outside and on their way to the car.

Still raining and blowing hard. Macklin barely noticed. The only thing on his mind right then was being out of that house, away from the palpable enmity among those four strangers.

FOUR

IN THE CAR JAY said, "Christ, that was unpleasant."

"You think so?"

"Don't you?"

"At least it was warm in there."

"Don't tell me you liked that bunch?"

"I didn't say that. No."

"I wish you hadn't agreed to drink with them."

"One drink, which I needed. The fire, too."

"I was uncomfortable the whole damn time."

Of course you were, Shelby thought. All kinds of people made him uncomfortable, strangers in particular. He hadn't always been like that. Once he'd been a people person, or tried to be even if he hadn't always been successful. Now he shied away at every opportunity, made excuses to avoid contact with anyone except old friends like Ben Coulter. Afraid of being hurt, which in her mind translated to being afraid of living. She was just the opposite. She liked people for the most part. Found even the odd ones like the Lomaxes and the Deckers interesting, not that she'd want to spend any more time in their company. It *had* gotten a little unpleasant in there toward the last.

Jay was backing out of the driveway onto the lane. "The way they kept sniping at each other," he said. "You could've cut the tension with a knife."

"The storm, strangers showing up. Too much to drink and getting on each other's nerves."

"And Lomax with that gun. Who did he think we were, home invaders?"

"He didn't threaten us with it, did he?"

"You know how I feel about guns."

"Yes," she said, "I know."

"The only half normal one was Claire," he said. "But she didn't really give a damn about getting to know us. Buffers. That's why she invited us to stay."

"Buffers?"

"Afraid something ugly, maybe violent was going to happen and us being there would diffuse it."

"You're exaggerating, Jay."

"No. I'm not."

"All right. Whatever."

He eased the car along the rainswept lane. The wiper on the passenger's side of the windshield seemed to have gone out of whack; it arced in little stuttering jerks, smearing more than clearing the glass. Another thing to be fixed, Shelby thought, another drain on their finances. Like the dryer that was about to give out, and the sink drain that kept clogging up, and the automatic garage door opener that no longer worked, and all the other little things that kept going wrong.

Their situation wouldn't have gotten so bad if Jay had been able to find work. It wasn't that he hadn't tried; it was the lousy economy and the fact that he was either overqualified for this job or underqualified for that one. Worst time of year to be looking, too; even the minimum-wage jobs were taken. His unemployment insurance would run out in another six months or so, and then what would they do? She made a decent salary, but she was already putting in maximum overtime, working the graveyard shift whenever she could for the extra pay. It was enough to keep them afloat, but without some additional income . . .

Jay said musingly, "I wonder what Paula meant."

"Meant about what?"

"After we sat down. She said something about wackos on the loose inside and out. Inside, yes, but why 'out'?"

"Smart-ass remark. She and her husband made a lot of them."

"Didn't sound like wisecracking to me."

"Well, she wasn't being cryptic, either, if that's what you're thinking."

"Not cryptic, just . . . I don't know. It seemed funny, that's all."

Sometimes he could be exasperating, the way he kept picking at things. First the deputy sheriff earlier and now the Lomaxes and the Deckers. "Why does it bother you so much?"

"Part of the tension in there."

"That's not what I meant. I meant why does the way the four of them acted bother you so much?"

"I don't know, it just does."

Well, she knew why. And so did he, even if he wouldn't admit it. Being confronted with other people's marital conflicts had sharpened his awareness of the conflicts in their marriage. Hit too close to home. She'd felt it, too, but she had the capacity to keep it in perspective.

She said, "Will you please just forget about it? We'll probably never see any of them again."

"What if they invite us to spend New Year's Eve with them?"

"They won't."

"Damn well say no if they do."

Back at the cottage now, turning in under the carport. The power was still out—naturally. Inside, the damp and the chill had taken over again; in the darkness, the dank, musty smell had a subterranean quality, like the inside of a sea cave. Quickly, guided by the flashlight, Shelby rounded up half a dozen candles from the supply closet and lit the wicks. Jay took the matches and got the fire going while she distributed the candles to each of the rooms.

Most of the ice in the martini pitcher was unmelted; that was how cold it was in there. She hesitated, looking into the pitcher. Enough for another glass. Usually two was her limit, but tonight, after that godawful four-hour drive and the bizarre twenty minutes or so at the Lomax place, she decided she was entitled to a little overindulgence.

The old Dorothy Parker quatrain popped into her head as she was pouring her glass full.

I like to have a martini,
Two at the very most.
After three I'm under the table,
After four I'm under my host.

Uh-uh, she thought, not tonight. Not under the table, and definitely not under Jay. Three martinis spaced out over an hour and a half weren't going to get her hammered or make her amorous. Still, she'd better eat something after she finished this one. It had been more than seven hours since the light, late lunch they'd had before leaving home.

Jay had the fire blazing now, the flames painting the darkness with a flickering red-orange glow. He said as he came over to her, "Better go easy. That's three on an empty stomach."

"I know how many I've had."

"I didn't mean it that way. Just making a comment."

The comment being that she was drinking too much lately. Well, he was right, she was. And until he'd suddenly slacked off before Christmas, so was he. Another indication that the marriage was in trouble—their mutual reliance on alcohol to get them through their evenings alone together. Maybe that was why he'd mostly quit after all: subtle pressure to get her to do the same. His noncommunicative way of trying to shore up the crumbling foundation of their relationship.

Sorry, sweetie, she thought, it's not working.

He said, "Let's get warm and then I'll make us something to eat."

"The good-cold casserole we brought with us?"

"Well, I had to tell them something to get us out of there," he said defensively. "No way we were going to eat with those people."

She'd meant the casserole comment as a mild joke, and he'd taken it as a rebuke for lying. As she'd taken his reminder about three martinis on an empty stomach as implied criticism. Each of them guilty of misreading the other, something that hadn't happened in the days when the foundation had been solid, that happened all too often now.

Was there any real chance of saving the marriage, bringing back the closeness they'd once shared? He might want to save it, but did she? Sometimes she thought yes, sometimes no, and sometimes she wondered if saving it was worth the effort. She still cared for him, but how much of that caring was love and a genuine need to be with him, and how much simple compassion, habit, inertia? She didn't know, couldn't make up her mind. One thing she did know: the degrees of separation between them were widening into an unbridgeable chasm. If the marriage did have a chance to survive, something major had to change—direction, communication, something. And soon, very soon.

No question a split would be difficult. She'd miss Jay; you couldn't love and live with a man for twelve years and not be left with an unfilled hole. But she'd get along all right. With or without Dr. Douglas Booth or any other male. She was resilient, more than capable of taking care of herself. She'd been taking care of people all her life. Mom, after Dad all of a sudden decided he preferred the bosom of somebody else's family to his own—first because of Mom's drinking, then full-time when the breast cancer was diagnosed, forcing her to quit school and alter her plans for a career as a health care worker. Jay the past few years. All the victims she'd had brief contact with on her job. And she'd come through all of that without too many scars, too many neuroses. Oh, yes, she was very good at taking care of people, herself included most of the time.

But Jay wasn't; he had to have somebody to count on, lean on. Somebody strong. Well, if they did go their separate ways, he wouldn't have too much trouble finding a suitable replacement . . . Yes, he would, why try to kid herself? A beaten-down man with low self-esteem wasn't exactly an ideal catch for any woman except a controlling or maternal one, neither of which was the type he needed.

Face it, Shelby, she thought. The woman he needs is you. And the crux of the problem is, you're tired of the burden and the responsibility.

She sat with her drink in a chair drawn up close to the fire while Jay

put together a meal in the kitchen. The spreading heat took away some of
the damp mustiness and, along with the effects of the gin, warmed her
again. Outside the wind had risen, buffeting the cottage with angry gusts,
but in here, with the fire and the candlelight, it was almost cozy. Almost.
Three martinis on an empty stomach could make any surroundings seem
tolerable, as long as there was enough light to keep the darkness at bay.

They ate sandwiches and stewed tomatoes in front of the fire, neither
of them saying much. That had always been one of the good things about
their relationship, the ability to sit together in companionable silence. Even
when they argued or fought, they seldom raised their voices. Nor had they
ever indulged in public bickering and name-calling, like the Lomaxes and
the Deckers; that kind of open hostility was foreign to both their natures.
A little private sniping now and then, sure, but what couple didn't do that?
Jay had his faults, but basically he was a quiet, gentle man. A good man. If
only he wasn't so infuriatingly introverted. And withdrawing deeper into
himself every day. That, too, as much as the string of failures and setbacks, as much as the burden and responsibility of looking out for him,
was what was slowly killing the marriage.

Bedtime. She took two lighted candles into the master bedroom, went
back to get a third. The fire's warmth didn't reach in there, but the bed,
at least, was covered with two blankets and a thick down comforter.

The adjoining bathroom was small and chilly. She took one of the
candles in there and made short work of changing and of using the toilet. When she came out, Jay was already in bed with the comforter pulled
up to his chin. She said as she got in beside him, "Whoever buys the toilet paper for this place has a sadistic streak."

"Poor quality?"

"Like sandpaper."

"Probably Ben. He didn't have much money when we were in college.
Thrifty about everything in those days."

"Nobody should be thrifty when it comes to their asses."

Jay burst out laughing. She gave him a look, and then realized how in-
dignant she'd sounded and laughed with him. Echo of the good early
days, when they'd laughed often together.

There was a sag in the middle of the mattress, so that when she turned on her side he slipped down against her back. The bed was too small to move away; she lay still, feeling the heat from his body, hoping he wouldn't turn and try to arouse her. He didn't. Within minutes his breathing told her he was asleep.

But he was restless tonight; his arms and legs kept twitching. Often enough that was a sign that he would have his nightmare. The same nightmare over and over—that was all he'd ever say about it. Whatever it was, it must be terrifying. He'd wake himself and her up with moans, little whimpers, then outcries that were close to screams. And he'd be soaked in sweat, shaky, his pulse rate so accelerated he had trouble catching his breath. She hoped it wouldn't happen tonight. The pain sounds he made and the sudden wrenching from sleep were bad enough, but the way his heart beat so rapidly for so long afterward was cause for alarm. So was the little hitch every few beats even when he was at rest.

Shelby could hear the hitch now as he slept. It was probably nothing but simple arrhythmia, as his shortness of breath was probably nothing but the result of being out of shape. But they and the too-rapid pulse rate could also be symptoms of angina or some other form of heart disease.

The first time she'd noticed the hitch, she'd suggested he see his doctor for a checkup and an EKG. He'd said he would, but as far as she knew he hadn't done it. She'd have to prod him again. Abnormalities were nothing to slough off, even in a man of thirty-five. She'd seen and treated too many coronary victims; watched three die on the way to the hospital ER, one of them a man in his late twenties.

One more thing to worry about . . .

FIVE

THE STORM BLEW ITSELF out sometime during the night. The wind was still yammering but there was no rain when Macklin got up and looked out through the bedroom window blinds. Heavy overcast, and a light fog swirling in among the pines and other trees that separated the cottage from the big estate to the south. Shelby was still asleep. He put on his new robe—her Christmas present to him this year—and went into the bathroom to use the toilet and splash his face with cold water. He hadn't slept well; he felt logy and tight all over, as if his skin had somehow shrunk during the night. At least what sleep he'd had had been dreamless.

He padded into the kitchen to see if the power had come back on. It had—a relief. He found coffee, set the pot brewing, then turned on the baseboard heater and raised the blinds over the mullioned windows that faced seaward. The ocean's surface was strewn with deer-tail whitecaps and huge fans of kelp. Below the unkempt lawn that sloped down to the bluff edge, part of the cove below was visible—spume geysering over a collection of offshore rocks each time one of the incoming waves broke. Ben had told him there was a rock-and-sand beach that ran the full length of the inlet, flanked by rocky headlands, accessible only to the three cliff-side homes. Maybe later, if the weather held, he and Shelby would go down there and check it out. One thing they had in common was the beach-comber gene.

In the kitchen again, he took out the breakfast fixings they'd brought with them, put together a Florentine omelette, readied six strips of bacon for broiling in the oven, sliced English muffins. Cooking was a source of pleasure for him, always had been, and he was good at it. For a time, after college, he'd thought about enrolling in one of the better culinary academies, learning how to be a quality chef, but he'd never followed through. Maybe if he had . . .

No, hell, he'd known back then that he wasn't cut out to be a chef. Restaurant owner was more suited to his abilities, or so he'd believed. He understood well-prepared food, he had managerial skills, all he'd lacked was the capital. Five years of dull work in the restaurant supply business, with every extra penny of his and Shelby's incomes saved, plus the cash from an affordable mortgage on the house Shel had inherited from her mother, and they'd taken the plunge.

Macklin's Grotto. Fine Seafood Specialties. A prime location in Morgan Hill, small but with an intimate atmosphere; a well-regarded chef trained in one of the better Manhattan restaurants, a menu that featured fresh fish and shellfish dishes, and the best cioppino he'd ever tasted. How could it miss being successful?

Except that it had. Oh, not in the beginning; business had been good the first year, with plenty of repeat customers and new ones brought in by word-of-mouth recommendation. But then the economy had begun to sag and people were less inclined to spend their money eating out. Arturo, the chef, had quit to take a better-paying job in San Francisco, and the best replacement Macklin could find for him hadn't been nearly as ac- complished or creative. Empty tables even on the weekends, cash reserves running out and bills piling up. And then the death kiss—the woman cus- tomer who'd slipped on a piece of salmon in cream sauce dropped by a careless waiter and cracked a bone in her wrist. Their insurance company had paid the medical and settlement bills, dropped them cold immediately afterward. And there was no way he could get another policy without paying an unaffordable high-risk premium.

Three years of living his dream, only one of them really good. Then back into the restaurant supply business as a glorified office manager at

Conray Foods—a mediocre job, but one that paid reasonably well. And then after a year and a half, with no warning, out on his ass and into line at the unemployment office.

And once the unemployment insurance maxed out at seventy-nine weeks, or more likely, was suspended sometime after the first of the year? It wouldn't make much difference in the short haul. But in the long haul . . . then what? Wasn't likely to be any kind of decent job for a man his age, with his limited skills and experience and health issues. He'd be lucky to get minimum-wage dregs: busboy at Burger King, grocery bagger at Safeway, newspaper deliveryman if there were still newspapers to be delivered. Some future. Some hope to offer Shelby.

What was that line from *Body Heat*? Something about the shit coming down so heavy sometimes you feel like wearing a hat. Right. Only with him, it'd have to be a ten-gallon Texas Stetson—

Feeling sorry for himself again. Knock it off, Macklin. Your life is what it is—period. Nobody to blame but the gods or whoever runs the universe, if anybody or anything does. Accept it. Be a man.

Grow up, be a man.

Pop's voice, echoing in his memory. Harold P. Macklin—always Harold, never Harry or Hal. Sporting goods salesman and habitual gambler who'd lost far more than he won at poker, horse races, blackjack, and the sports books in Tahoe and Reno. Cold, distant, domineering. Lousy husband, lousy father. Ruled Ma and his two sons with an iron fist and an acid tongue.

Stop acting like a goddamn baby, Jayson. Grow up, be a man.

I'm sick and tired of answering your stupid questions. What do I look like, an encyclopedia?

Cooking? That's woman's work. What are you, a faggot?

Sometimes you make me wish to Christ I'd had a vasectomy the year before you were born.

He remembered the October day when he was fifteen, the school principal taking him out of his English class to tell him that both his parents were dead in a highway accident. On their way home from one of their frequent trips to Reno, Tom and him left in the care of Aunt Carolyn or to fend for themselves as they grew older; Pop driving too fast and losing control on an icy stretch near Donner Summit, both of them killed outright. He'd cried for Ma, but not for the old man. Never shed a tear for him, never missed him. Seldom even thought of him, except for a teenage vow to be a damn sight better man. And yet here he was, his father's son in the only way that really counted.

Harold P. Macklin, Jayson L. Macklin—a couple of losers.

The coffee was ready. He could hear Shelby stirring around in the bedroom, awakened by the aroma. He turned on the broiler, started an omelette large enough for two. He wasn't hungry, but maybe she was.

Her mood this morning seemed better than yesterday's: She had a smile for him when she came out. Quiet at the table, but when she did say something it had an upbeat ring. At least she was making an effort.

"I should go into Seacrest," he said after they finished eating, "pick up a few things at the grocery, fill the gas tank. Want to come along?"

"I don't think so."

"Won't take long."

"I'll find something to do here," she said. Meaning she preferred her own company to his. "See if you can get a new wiper blade while you're there. The one on the passenger side started sticking last night."

"Yeah, I noticed. I'll take care of it."

Macklin waited until ten thirty before leaving, figuring that the grocery store and garage would be open by then—if they were open at all this time of year. He didn't relish the prospect of having to hunt down groceries and a new wiper blade somewhere other than Seacrest; the nearest town in either direction was fifteen miles.

He was backing out of the carport onto the lane when the angry blare of a horn sounded close behind him. He jammed on the brakes just as a car whipped past, coming too fast from the direction of the Lomax property and narrowly missing the Prius's rear end. Dark blue four-door sedan with a woman at the wheel—Claire Lomax or Paula Decker, he couldn't tell which in the brief look he had before the car disappeared.

The storm had done minor damage in places: a bishop pine splintered in the woods that bordered Ocean Point Lane; a small rockslide along

Highway 1 halfway to Seacrest; a small chunk of cliffside eroded away where the highway ran close to the edge, leaving a long scar down to the sea. He remembered reading somewhere that problems like this were common on this part of the coast during El Niño winters. Not a place you'd want to live year-round unless you craved isolation or were born with a pioneer spirit.

By daylight, Seacrest didn't seem nearly so cheerless. Attractive little wide spot in the highway, with sweeping ocean views and forested mountain slopes for an inland backdrop. Signs of activity here and there, and both the grocery store and the service station/garage open for business. Get the shopping out of the way first, he thought, and pulled into the grocery parking lot.

One other car was parked there—the dark blue sedan. He knew it was the same one because when he brought up next to it, Paula Decker came walking out of the store wrapped in a black coat with a fur collar. She had a package of cigarettes in one hand and was tearing at the cellophane wrapping with the other.

There was no way he could avoid contact with her, short of hiding by lying down across the seat. The hell with it, he thought, and got out as she approached. She didn't see him at first, intent on the cigarettes; her mouth was compressed into a tight, angry line. He sidestepped, thinking maybe he could get past her after all, but then her head came up and she stopped and looked at him, at the Prius, at him again. Whatever she was upset about, it wasn't the near miss back on Ocean Point Lane. Her gaze held neither anger nor animosity.

"Oh," she said, "hello. Mackson, isn't it?"

"Macklin. Jay Macklin."

"Right. I almost hit you back there on the lane."

"My fault. I should've been paying closer attention."

In the cold light of day, with an obvious hangover, Paula wasn't half as attractive as she'd seemed the night before. Skin even blotchier and less healthy looking, bagged and bloodshot eyes, a network of fine lines etched across and alongside her upper lip. Her brown hair had a stringy, tangled look, as though she'd used her fingernails on it instead of a comb.

She ripped the package open, slid a filter-tip out and into one corner of her mouth. "Got a light?"

"No. I don't smoke."

"Yeah, well, my asshole husband doesn't like me to smoke, either. Screw him." She opened the purse slung over her shoulder, rummaged up a gold lighter and fired the weed. "Ahh," she said through a spew of carcinogens. "I may just smoke this whole goddamn pack on the way to Santa Rosa."

"You're going home?"

"That's right. Home not so sweet home, but at least it's safe. There's more than one wacko running around loose up here, by God."

"What do you mean?"

"Just what I said. I don't know why I came in the first place. I should've known better."

"What about the others? Are they staying?"

"I don't know and I don't care. I wouldn't care if they all jumped off the cliff drunk on New Year's Eve. I used to think my big brother was a great guy, now I can't stand the sight of him. Claire's a nasty little bitch and Gene . . . he'd fuck a woodpile if he thought it had a snake in it."

What could you say to that? Macklin didn't even try.

"I'm not stupid, for Christ's sake," Paula said. "Not anymore, I'm not. Enough is enough. You wouldn't happen to know a good divorce lawyer, would you?"

"Sorry, no."

"Well, I'm going to need one. I can take a lot, I *have* taken a lot, but some things you just . . . Oh, shit, why am I telling you all this? You don't care. Why should you? We're just a bunch of strangers to you."

Right, Macklin thought. A bunch of screwed-up strangers.

"Just getting myself more worked up, is all." Paula exhaled another stream of smoke, dropped the butt and ground it under her heel. "Forget it—I'm outta here. Have a nice life, Ray."

"Jay."

"Whatever," she said, and got into the sedan, and wheeled it around and out of the lot in a spray of gravel and a shriek of tires.

Good riddance, Macklin thought. He hoped her husband and the Lomaxes decided to leave, too. The more dealings he had with any of that bunch, the less he liked the idea of them being neighbors for the next three days.

SIX

After Jay left for Seacrest, Shelby rattled around the cottage trying to find something to do with herself. One of those loose-ends mornings when no activity seemed to appeal to her. They hadn't brought the laptop with them; the only e-mail they were likely to get between Christmas and New Year's was spam and neither of them was much for surfing the Net, though she wouldn't have minded doing a little of that right now. Besides, Ben had told Jay that the only Internet service available from the cottage was dial-up.

She poked through the bookcase and the CDs. Aside from Kate's historical romances, and a handful of Harry Potter titles that would belong to the Coulters' twelve-year-old son, Derek, the hodgepodge assortment of paperbacks might have been indiscriminately swept off a thrift shop shelf; the only one of even mild interest was a bestselling suspense novel. There were quite a few classical CDs, her preference, but she wasn't in the mood for music either. And it was too early in the day to watch a movie.

Well?

Well, maybe a few minutes on the phone with Mary Ellen would put her in a better mood. She'd always been able to talk to Mary Ellen, her best friend since high school in Aptos. They'd both attended UC Santa Cruz, too, only Mary Ellen had stayed the course and graduated with a degree in history, a subject she now taught at a private school in Los

Gatos. It had been Mary Ellen who'd introduced her to Jay at an off-campus party in their sophomore year.

The only problem with the phone call idea was that her cellular didn't work up here. She tried it inside and then outside on the patio—no signal, satellite dead zone. And didn't that just figure? She could use the Coulters' land line, if it was working, but she didn't want to run up Ben's phone bill with long-distance minutes. He probably wouldn't mind or let her pay him back, but she didn't believe in sponging off other people. Four days' free use of the cottage was as far as she'd go, acceptable because it was a gesture of friendship that didn't involve money.

She noticed then that the wood box was mostly empty; they'd used up a lot of firewood last night. No need to wait for Jay to fill it up. She wasn't feeble and she still had her coat and gloves on from the cell phone try.

There were a pair of sheds tucked away behind the carport, squat structures with slanted sheet metal roofs. One had a padlocked door, probably a utility or gardening shed; the other's door was closed by a rusted metal bolt thrust through a hasp. Inside that one were rows of neatly stacked logs and kindling, and a canvas wood carrier to make transportation easier. She loaded and lugged the carrier inside three times—more than enough firewood to last the rest of the day.

When she finished rebolting the woodshed door, she thought she might as well do a little exploring and made her way down the slope. The sky was overcast and there were wisps of fog fingering among the trees to the north and south; the wind had died down and the day wasn't as cold as she'd expected. Gopher holes pocked the weedy open space, some of them filled with rainwater. As she made her way down, she had a fairly clear whitewater view through the trees: waves breaking and creaming over the offshore and inshore rocks. The sea was the color of pewter, spotted with baby whitecaps.

Near the bottom there was a footworn path that wound through patches of manzanita and Scotch broom, past a couple of bare-branched trees that looked dead and probably were. The path ended at a short wooden platform clinging to the bluff's edge, enclosed on three sides by waist-high railings, anchored to a rock ledge on concrete posts crosshatched with boards. It looked unstable, but when she ventured a few steps onto it, she found that it was solidly constructed.

Part of the cove was visible from there, south to where the land curved outward to the waterline, north to where tall jumbles of rock hid the inlet below the Lomax property; a piece of the perimeter headland was visible, but not the house itself. The beach, what Shelby could see of it, was about a hundred yards long and fifty yards wide at its widest point— mostly a jumble of small broken rocks strewn with driftwood and brown, bulbous kelp; tidepools, leftovers from last night's high waves, glistened here and there. She could smell the kelp, a faintly rank, briny odor on the light wind.

A V-line of pelicans came into view from the south, skimming the ocean's surface on their way to whatever fishing grounds they frequented. When they were gone, she found herself gazing straight out to sea—and remembering an exchange she'd had with Jay some years back, on a beach down near Pescadero. They'd been looking out to sea as she was doing now, and she'd said that what the vast expanse of water made her think of was what lay on the other side, all the different faraway lands and cultures that were touched and surrounded by it. And he'd responded that what it made him think of was how massive and empty it was, and how tiny you'd feel if you were out in the middle of it all alone in a small boat.

There in a nutshell was the fundamental difference between them, the disparity in how they thought and felt and looked at the world—the broad view versus the narrow view, the positive versus the negative.

Steps had been cut into the cliffside to the left of the platform, some carved out of bare rock and some made of wood, with a sectioned handrail following them down to the cove below—a winding, gradual descent through a natural declivity, a distance of maybe 150 feet. Rain puddles had collected on some of the steps, but the descent didn't look too precarious . . . as long as that handrail was stable. Shelby went to the wooden landing at the top of the steps for a closer look. The railing seemed as solidly anchored as the platform.

She went down a few steps, experimentally. The footing wasn't bad at all in her thick-soled running shoes. She kept on going.

At the bottom she picked her way over the rocky shingle to the south. Once she paused to peer into a tidepool, but there was a murkiness to the water and she couldn't see much through it. The wind was little more than a medium-cool breeze down here, the beach sheltered by the high curving bluffs, the threads of fog drifting high overhead. The tide had started to ebb and as she neared the waterline she could see out to where exposed shelves of rock sloped off into deeper water. There'd be abalone out there, and in the early morning hours, divers off boats anchored offshore— legitimate abalone fishermen in season, poachers year-round.

The sea's salt-heavy breath sharpened her thoughts, the same old ones replaying on a stuttery loop but now with even greater clarity. She felt a sense of . . . what? Not exactly urgency, but a prodding restlessness, a growing need to stop waffling and start making decisions.

Jay and the marriage.

Yes, and Douglas, too.

So far she had resisted sleeping with him. A casual affair was the last thing she wanted or needed. But the temptation was strong. He was an attractive man, easy to talk to, a good listener, and he seemed to understand her in ways Jay never had. She hadn't had to tell him her marriage was in trouble; he'd picked up on all the signs—the bitterness, the loneliness, the faint undercurrent of tension that came from a love fading, maybe dying. He'd broached the subject himself the last time she'd seen him, over coffee after they'd both pulled all-nighters just before Christmas.

"Are you happy, Shelby?"

"What makes you ask that?"

"I think you know. You're not, are you?"

"Does it matter that much to you?"

"Yes, it does. I care about you. If there's anything I can do . . ."

"Such as what? Advice?"

"I'm not Dear Abby. Or an advice nurse."

"What, then? Lend a sympathetic ear, offer a shoulder to cry on?"

"If that's what you need."

"Or a different bed to lie on, in case that's what I need?"

"Don't be cynical, okay? I'm not going to hit on you—I don't operate that way. If all I wanted was a casual affair, I'd've made a pass long before this."

"What do you want, Douglas?"

"For you not to be unhappy."

He'd meant it. Meant everything he'd said, including not hitting on her. He hadn't pressured her in any way, at least not overtly.

But quiet persistence was a kind of pressure. So was the way he'd looked at her that morning, with low-burning heat showing beneath his empathy. There was no question that he felt the same sexual attraction for her that she felt for him. He really wouldn't be satisfied with a casual affair any more than she would; he wasn't that type of man. If she slept with him, he'd want a commitment to a relationship that was at least semipermanent. Was she ready for that, after all the years with Jay? And with a man she'd only known for a few months?

Evidently not, or she'd already have done something about it.

What was it she did want? To be not unhappy, yes—but what would make her happy again? For the marriage to work the way it had in the beginning? Or to be free, not just of Jay but of Dr. Douglas Booth as well? No complications, no pressures, just time alone to rebuild a life on her own terms?

Maybe.

Maybe the solution was to make a quick, clean break. Walk away from Jay, and from Douglas, too. Walk away from the known into the unknown. Could she do that? Six months ago, even three months ago, the answer would have been no. Now . . . it wouldn't be easy, but she was pretty sure she could.

The rocks close to the water's edge were coated with lichen that looked slippery; she avoided them, poking among the storm detritus farther up. Shells, all broken by the pounding action of the surf. The remains of a dead seagull. A crushed beer can. Two plastic water bottles. A chunk of white Styrofoam that might have come from the lid of an ice chest. Large and small logs, splintered tree limbs, bits and pieces of driftwood sculpted by the elements into different shapes, some of which seemed almost artistically designed.

Just ahead was the land barrier that separated this section of beach from the part below the big estate. At low tide you could make your way around the outthrust of granite, but the footing looked precarious now. Better not risk it.

She went back past the cliffside steps and on up the beach to the north. The shoreline was sandy in places here, but there were also the large jumbled rocks she'd seen from the platform and a series of smooth, up-swept limestone shelves. She climbed over one of the larger shelves, where a runnel from an underground freshwater stream poured out of an open-ing in the cliff wall. When she hopped down on the other side, she was facing a pair of high, rounded boulders like nippleless breasts with a nar-row cleavage between them. She squeezed through the passage—and came to an abrupt standstill.

A woman was sitting hunched on another shelf a short distance ahead, staring out to sea.

Even in profile, Shelby recognized her immediately: Claire Lomax.

Either she made a noise or the woman sensed her presence. Claire turned, saw her, and twisted around onto one hip, her body hunched and one hand flat on the rock, like a startled cat about to run. Past her, in the distance, Shelby could see the seaward quarter of the Lomax house against the backdrop of the headland above. The beach in between was mostly open; there was nobody else in sight.

Claire held her startled-cat pose for three or four seconds, then she seemed to sag a little, as if with resignation. She slid her body around so that she was facing Shelby.

No choice then but to go ahead and approach her. Claire wore a sheep-skin jacket with the collar pulled up and a tie-dyed scarf tied around her blonde hair, so that her face was a pale oval in between. Only not completely pale: there were discolored marks on it today—marks that took on definition as Shelby neared and that explained the woman's ap-parent impulse to run away. Split upper lip. Inch-long abrasion on her right cheek, and above that a yellowing bruise that would soon darken and spread and blacken the eye.

SEVEN

WHOEVER OWNED THE SEACREST grocery store had made maximum use of a small space: It was packed to the brim with shelves, bins, racks arranged in a mazelike fashion, the aisles so narrow that one of any two people passing with handbaskets would have to turn sideways. A heavyset, gray-haired woman stood behind the checkout counter; the only other occupant, a skinny man in a soiled apron, presided over a meat and deli section.

Macklin smiled and nodded at the woman; she gave him a blank-faced stare in return. Her eyes followed him as he picked up a basket and moved around the store. So did the man's when he passed by the meat counter.

Wariness again. Mistrust of strangers. Or was he just imagining it? No, dammit, he could see it and he could feel it, just like last night with that deputy. What was the matter with people around here? Sparsely populated rural area, yes, but it was also a tourist destination in better-weather months. And this was the Christmas season. Hard to believe holiday cheer and goodwill had become a lost concept on this part of the coast.

He located matches, picked out vegetables, ordered a fresh crab cracked and cleaned from the reticent counterman. The woman watched him set the basket down on the checkout counter, then quit making eye contact as she rang up the items. Frustration more than anything else prodded him into breaking the silence.

"Some storm last night."

It was a few seconds before she said, "Worse one on the way."

"Really? When?"

"Sometime tomorrow afternoon."

"Long-range weather forecast was for light rain."

"Wrong as usual. Big storm—high winds, heavy rain."

"Do you think it'll last long?"

"Depends. No way to tell until it gets here." Eyes the color of milk chocolate briefly met his. "You staying in the area?"

"My wife and I, yes."

"Seacrest?"

"No. A friend's cottage a few miles north."

"Place well stocked? Plenty of firewood, extra candles?"

"Why? Is there likely to be another power failure?"

"Wouldn't be surprised. Happens often enough when it storms heavy."

"A long outage like last night?"

"Had one lasted four days, a couple of winters ago. You sure you have everything you need?"

"I think so. Yes."

She shrugged, took his money, gave him change—all without looking at him again. He said, "Happy New Year," as he picked up the grocery sack, but she didn't respond. He could feel her eyes on him again as he walked out.

More of the same at the service station. The mechanic on duty in the garage, a sinewy man in his forties wearing grease-stained overalls with the name *Earl* stitched across one pocket, was civil enough but in a cool, watchful way.

"Wiper blades for a Prius?" he said. "Can't help you there, mister. Don't carry any that'll fit. You can get 'em in Fort Bragg, if you're going that far."

"I'm not. Staying nearby for a few days."

"That right? Well, I suppose I could order a set for you. Have 'em here tomorrow or Saturday, latest."

"I'd appreciate it."

Macklin went with him into a cluttered office, where Earl wrote up an order and he paid a deposit. When they came out again, a mud-spattered white pickup, its bed covered by a blue tarpaulin, was just pulling in behind where the Prius was parked at the forward of the two gas pumps. A gray-bearded oldster in a heavy pea jacket climbed out of the cab. Earl said, "Hey, Walter," in friendlier tones and went over to join him.

Macklin slid his credit card into the pump's fast-pay slot, then opened the Prius's gas cap and inserted the hose nozzle. Earl and the bearded man, Walter, were talking now and making no effort to keep their voices down. Words carried clearly to Macklin on the cold, salt-laden wind.

"No, I didn't hear," Walter was saying. "I been over to my daughter's in Vacaville, just got back last night. Where'd they find this one?"

"Down by Manchester."

"Oh, Jesus. That's another one too close for comfort."

"Tell me about it."

"They sure it's the same bastard?"

"Sure enough. Makes four, but could be others ain't been found yet. Now they're calling him the Coastline Killer."

"Goddamn media." Walter smacked a fisted hand against his leg. "Who was it this time?"

"Delivery driver for one of the beer outfits—Ned Trotter. I didn't know him, but June over at the store did."

"Isn't he the guy got arrested for abalone poaching last year?"

"Yeah, and he was at it again. Sackful in his truck."

"Shot like the others?"

"Once through the head and then laid out neat. They didn't find the bullet this time, but from the wound they figure it's the same gun."

"How you know that?"

"Deputy Ferguson. He come by about an hour ago."

"Three five seven Magnum, what do you bet?"

"If they know for sure what kind, Ferguson wouldn't say."

"When'd it happen? Yesterday?"

"No, that's when they found the body. Day before, day after Christmas—early morning, probably right after he finished poaching."

Macklin set the catch on the nozzle, moved over to where the two men were standing. "Sorry to butt in," he said, "but I couldn't help overhearing. Four people shot to death?"

Now Walter was looking at him the way the woman in the store and Earl had, the way the deputy had last night. There was a little silence before Earl said, "Four that they know about."

"But not all in the same vicinity?"

"Up and down the coast. First you heard about it, huh?"

"I'm not from around here. My wife and I live in Cupertino."

"Don't you pay attention to the news down in Cupertino?" Walter asked.

"Not crime news, no."

"Well, maybe it's time you started."

"Papers made a big deal out of the first two in July," Earl said. "Two kids on the beach down near Fort Ross. Both shot in the head. Sick bastard laid 'em out naked in a sleeping bag afterward."

"Oh. That case."

"Rings a bell now, huh?"

It did. He'd skimmed an article about that bizarre double homicide, just hadn't made the connection. July was months past and Fort Ross was a long way down the coast from Seacrest.

"The police couldn't find a motive," he said.

"That's right. Still can't."

"Psychos don't need motives," Walter said.

Macklin asked, "And there've been two others since?"

Earl said, "Number three late November, up on the Navarro River. And now number four down by Manchester."

"Random victims and locations, then."

"How it looks."

"All outdoors? I mean, whoever's doing it doesn't break into people's houses . . ."

"Not so far. But that don't mean he won't get it into his head to start."

"Police think he lives somewhere along the coast?"

"Maybe. Might be a second-homer."

"My money's on a Mexican," Walter said, "one of them illegals we got roaming around here. I never did trust those people. They get drunk or hopped up, I wouldn't put anything past 'em."

Earl glanced sideways at Macklin. "Ferguson's got another idea: somebody that comes and stays a few days in one place or another, then goes back home until the next time."

"I've never been here before." The words sounded defensive even to Macklin. "Well, ten years ago, on a driving trip my wife and I took."

"Wasn't accusing you of anything, mister."

"I know you weren't. I was just . . ." He shook his head and said, "I hope they catch him before he kills somebody else."

"Damn well better."

Macklin went back to finish with his fill-up. Well, now he knew the reason behind all the thinly veiled suspicion, the meaning of the cryptic exchange between the Deckers last night and Paula Decker's comment this morning. A wacko on the loose along the north coast, shooting people at random without apparent motive—no wonder the residents here were on edge. The Coastline Killer. More and more of that kind of lunacy these days, in rural as well as urban and suburban surroundings. Serial killers, crazies shooting up high schools and college campuses with automatic weapons, husbands snapping and taking out their families and anyone else who got in the way. Global lunacy, too: 9/11, suicide bombers, the ever-present threat of other vicious acts of terrorism. Lord, what a world this had become.

Was there any danger to Shelby and him? Potentially, yes, but so minimal as to be almost nonexistent. The latest shooting was just two days ago, and it had been several weeks between that one and each of the others. Brian Lomax might be worried enough to meet strangers who came knocking with a gun in his hand, but none of the killings had involved home invasion: you were bound to be safe locked inside a private cottage. There was a lot of Sonoma County and Mendocino County coast, too, some of it more isolated than this section. Whoever the Coastline Killer was, he could be anywhere along that two-county stretch—as far as fifty, sixty miles from here. Or somewhere else entirely by now.

If he told Shelby about the shootings, it might put an unnecessary strain on the rest of their stay. Or, worse, she might use it as an excuse to pressure him into cutting the time short, going on home. He couldn't let that happen.

All right, so he'd keep the news to himself. If the future played out as badly as he feared, what the hell else did he have to look forward to except these next few days?

EIGHT

Claire made no effort to hide the injuries to her face. One corner of her mouth twitched—a smile that wasn't a smile. "Pretty sight, aren't I," she said.

"I've seen worse," Shelby said.

"I'll bet you have."

"What happened?"

"I could tell you I fell, but you probably wouldn't believe me."

"Did you fall?"

The faint nonsmile again. Claire shifted her gaze back to the sea, but Shelby had the impression she wasn't really seeing the rumpled gray water. Different woman than the one who'd welcomed Jay and her last night. The anxious, overfriendly hostess was gone; this Claire Lomax was subdued, hurting, and more than a little scared. When she lifted one hand to finger her torn lip, it trembled noticeably.

"I like it out here," she said. "Even in weather like this. There's something . . . I don't know, soothing about the ocean."

Shelby said, "Look, it's none of my business. I'll just leave you alone—"

"No, don't." The blonde head swung back her way, a silent plea in the pearl-gray eyes. "I need somebody to talk to. Another woman who'll understand."

"What about your sister-in-law?"

"Gone. Packed up and left about an hour ago. I couldn't talk to her anyway. Not Paula." Claire sucked in her breath, blew it out as if it were smoke burning her lungs. "I didn't fall and I didn't walk into a door. You're a paramedic . . . you know what you're seeing."

All too well. She'd borne witness to the aftermath of domestic violence too many times. Seen the smashed and bloodied faces, the broken bones and torn flesh; heard the screams and the angry accusations and tearful lies and fumbling, stupid excuses. Some people, most but not all of them men, reverted to animals when they were drunk or stoned or just plain out of control.

"When did it happen?"

"Last night, not long after you and your husband left."

"What was the cause?"

"Brian thinks I've been having an affair."

Shelby resisted asking the obvious question. Instead she said, "Were you alone with him when he accused you?"

"No. Gene and Paula were there."

"Did Gene try to stop him?"

"Gene?" Claire laughed, but it hurt her mouth and she winced and cut it off. "He's a lover, not a fighter. Besides, he's got his own marital problems. You heard the way he and Paula were going at each other last night."

"Yes."

"Paula's not going to put up with it anymore. That's why she left this morning. Their marriage is over."

And you wish yours was, too, Shelby thought.

She asked, "Is Gene still here?"

"For now he is. If he decides to leave . . ."

"You'll be alone with your husband."

"For the next three days, because he's determined to stay through New Year's."

"And you're afraid he'll come at you again."

A gull wheeling overhead let out a sudden screeching cry, as if it were mimicking a shriek of pain; the sound caused Claire to jump, raise one hand as if to ward off a blow. "God," she said, "my nerves are shot."

"Has he done this before, beat you up?"

"Three or four times the last year or so. He wasn't like that the first few years we were married. He never touched me except when we made love. Then he . . . changed. Turned moody, distant. Angry all the time. He's always been jealous, but now . . ." She shook her head, winced, and touched her lip again.

"What changed him?"

"I don't know exactly. Job pressures, I suppose. The economy. He owes the bank a lot of money . . . he may lose his company. He couldn't stand that."

"That's no excuse for taking it out on you."

"I've told him that, more times than I can count. He doesn't listen to me, he doesn't seem to care what I think or feel anymore. All he cares about is his work, the environment, spending time in that house he built up on the bluff. He comes up here alone, sometimes for days on end. At least I think this is where he goes—he won't tell me. If I didn't know better, I'd think he was the one having an affair."

"But you're sure he isn't."

"Pretty sure." The gull shrieked again; this time Claire didn't seem to notice. "I used to love my life," she said. "You know, married to a wealthy man, expensive clothes, jewelry, a nice car, trips to Mexico and Hawaii. Now . . . sometimes now I fucking *hate* it."

Same here, Shelby thought. Sometimes.

She said, "You don't have to stay with him."

"I know. But if I leave . . ."

"You think he'll come after you?"

"He might. He doesn't like to lose what belongs to him."

"A woman doesn't *belong* to anybody but herself."

"Tell Brian that. He'll laugh in your face like he laughed in mine when I told him pretty much the same thing."

"Stay, and he'll keep on taking out his frustrations on you," Shelby said. She couldn't quite keep the anger she felt from threading her words. "Someday he's liable to hurt you a lot worse than he did last night."

"I know that, too. You don't think I like being afraid, do you?"

"Then why don't you leave?"

"I could tell you it's because I still love him, that I keep hoping he'll turn back into the man he used to be."

"But it wouldn't be the truth."

"No. I don't love him anymore, I'm scared to death of him."

"Then get out before it's too late."

"And go where? I don't have money of my own or anywhere to go."

"There are battered women's shelters."

"I couldn't stand a place like that. Besides, he'd find me and then things would be even worse—" She glanced up at the redwood-and-glass house on the bluff top, then gingerly eased herself off the shelf. "I'd better get back before he comes looking for me." The faint, empty smile. "He's liable to think I'm down here seducing your husband."

"Claire . . ."

"Yes?"

"If your brother-in-law does leave today, think about going with him."

"Oh, God, no, that's the last thing I'd do. Brian wouldn't allow it— it'd just set him off again if I tried."

Shelby didn't push it. Instead she said, "We'll be here until New Year's morning, if you want to talk again. Or need a ride anywhere for any reason."

Claire blinked at her. "You'd do that for somebody you barely know?"

"My job is helping people in trouble."

"Well . . . I appreciate it, I really do, but I'll be all right. I can handle Brian when he's sober. I won't let him drink as much as he did yesterday."

Famous last words. "The offer is good as long as we're here."

"Thanks." Claire started away, stopped and looked back. "It's helped, talking to you. I'm glad we met."

Shelby watched her walk away along the beach in slow, stiff strides. My God, she thought, the things we do to each other, the things we do to ourselves.

NINE

"I KNEW IT," MACKLIN SAID. "I knew Lomax was the kind of lowlife bastard who beats up on his wife. Didn't I tell you there were bad vibes in that house?"

"Yes, you told me."

"I didn't like him the minute I laid eyes on him. Standing there with that gun in his hand— Christ! You don't suppose he'd use it on her, do you?"

"He might, with enough provocation. He's an angry, violent, abusive drunk. Unpredictable."

"Paula knows it, too. Probably another reason why she left."

"Probably."

"Did you say anything to Claire about the gun?"

"No. What could I say?"

"Well, she should be aware of the risk."

"She's aware of it," Shelby said. "She's not stupid."

"Then why doesn't she hide the gun somewhere? Or get rid of it— throw it into the ocean?"

"She's too afraid of doing anything that might set him off again. What she really needs to do is leave him and get a restraining order, but she's like so many battered wives—she just doesn't have the courage."

They were standing on the platform at the bluff's edge. Shelby hadn't been in the cottage when he got back from Seacrest; he'd come down here looking for her, found her just climbing the steps from the beach. The look on her face prompted him to ask what was wrong and she'd told him. And in turn he'd told her about his brief encounter with Paula Decker in Seacrest.

He said, "You think Claire has been having an affair?"

"She didn't say and I didn't ask."

"Paula called her a nasty little bitch."

"That doesn't mean anything. Paula's one herself. If Claire's been sleeping with somebody else, she was driven to it. I wouldn't blame her."

"Neither would I. A woman trapped in a lousy marriage has a right to—"

He broke off. Subtle shift from the impersonal to the personal in what he'd been about to say. Shelby was also a woman trapped in what was becoming, or in her eyes might have already become, a lousy marriage. Different kind of lousy, sure—he'd never raised a hand to her and never would—but just as unhappy. He didn't believe she'd cheat on him; he'd never once considered cheating on her. If she did, though, he couldn't blame her any more than she blamed Claire Lomax. But he didn't want to know. Ever. No matter what happened between them, he needed his bedrock beliefs intact, his memories untainted.

"Well, anyhow," he said, "I don't think we should have anything more to do with those people."

"I feel the same way. But if Claire comes to me for help, I'm not going to turn my back on her."

"I wouldn't expect you to."

"Let's go on up," Shelby said. "It's chilly out here."

Macklin made lunch for them from his Seacrest purchases: cracked crab, pasta salad, sourdough French bread. They didn't talk any more about the Lomaxes, or about much of anything else.

The afternoon passed in what seemed like stalled time. They played a couple of games of Scrabble, a board game they'd always enjoyed . . . he'd always enjoyed, anyway. Played mostly in silence. Shelby's mind clearly wasn't on it today, although she won the second game on the strength of a 66-point, triple-word, double-letter-V score with the word *quiver*.

She didn't want to play a third. He suggested they take a nap together; the look she gave him quashed that idea. What would she like to do then? She said she didn't know, what did he want to do? Paddy Chayefsky dialogue. I dunno, Marty, what do you feel like doing?

Oh yeah, they were having a great time. Some real spousal bonding going on here.

He sat there feeling frustrated and ineffectual as hell. What kind of man couldn't amuse his wife or himself, just kept on finding ways to bore the crap out of both of them?

This was something else he hated about himself, this nagging feeling of inadequacy. He'd had plenty of self-confidence once because there'd been more than a few things he'd been good at. School subjects—English, American lit, history, even math. Cooking. Baseball.

God yes, baseball.

The game had come easy to him, every phase of it—hitting, base running, fielding. He'd had a .373 average his first year at UC Santa Cruz, fifteen home runs and a dozen stolen bases. Been just as good if not better on defense—covered more ground, caught more balls than any outfielder on any team he'd played with, from Little League to college. Pro potential, no question, until the home-plate collision that blew out his knee and left him unable to run with any speed.

One catch he'd made his first year in college was forever sharp in his memory. Ninth inning, two out, Cal Poly with the bases loaded, Santa Cruz up by a run. Towering drive by their cleanup hitter that he saw all the way, as soon as it left the aluminum bat with that booming metallic clang. Fast and easy backward glide to the warning track at the center-field fence, and then up, up, he'd never jumped higher, must've been two feet off the ground when the ball smacked into the webbing of his glove, then his body slamming hard into the fence and the impact popping the ball out, but seeing that too as if it were happening in slow motion and snatching it in midair with his left hand as he was falling, cradling it against his chest when he hit the ground, rolling over and coming up holding the ball high like a trophy, and the ump making the out sign and the fans cheering and his teammates running toward him shouting his name . . . He'd been a big dog that day, he'd stood taller than the eight-foot fence that day.

Making love, that was another thing he was good at. No brag—simple fact. Not because he was one of these stallion types who equated sex with running a marathon race. Because the important thing to him was pleasing his partner; the better it was for her, the better it was for him. The night he'd lost his virginity, when he was a sophomore in high school, the girl had said to him afterward, "Wow! I can't believe it was your first time." And Shelby, their first time together: "Oh God, Jay, you're so gentle, it was so *good*." This wasn't empty flattery; she'd said similar things any number of other times before and after they were married. But not in so long now he couldn't remember the last time—

"Jay. Jay!"

". . . What?"

"Are you going to just sit there staring into space?"

"Sorry. No."

"What were you thinking about?"

"Nothing," he said. "Let's go down to the beach."

She wasn't enthusiastic about that, either, since she'd already been down there, but when he went to put on his coat she got up and joined him.

They avoided the northern part of the cove, made their way down to where the landmass marked the end of Ben's property. The tide was out and they were able to skirt around the point onto the beach below the big neighboring estate.

Quite a place, from what he could see of it through a long open crease in the cliffside. What must be the main house sprawled back behind a long redwood deck—two stories of weird angles and windows in different geometric shapes, all of it looking cobbled together as if from a collection of mismatched pieces. There was a kind of a dormer at one end that was almost as high as the backdrop of pines.

"Some architect's wet dream," Macklin said. "I'll bet Lomax hates it."

"Why would anyone build a home like that if they weren't going to live in it full time?"

"More money than good sense."

"It's a wonder the Coastal Commission approved the plans."

"With enough money you can get anything done."

"Well, we'll never know if that's true or not." Trace of bitterness in her voice? Hard to tell, with the wind yowling at them.

"No," he said. "I guess we never will."

They didn't stay long. The wind gained velocity, sweeping in vanguards from a wall of fog that was making up offshore. The sudden drop in temperature drove them back up the steps to the bluff top.

Just as they were coming onto the landing, there was a loud engine roar and a harsh clash of gears from out on the lane. Sports car, shooting past toward the highway—Decker's Porsche. Another grinding downshift, and the engine sound faded to silence.

Macklin said disgustedly, "Sweet car like that Boxster—Decker treats it the way he treats his wife, like crap."

"He must've decided to go home after all."

"Or off to see one of his girlfriends, or to the store for more booze."

"If he's going to Santa Rosa, I'd like to think Claire's with him."

"Probably not, from what she told you today."

"No, probably not."

Inside the cottage, he stacked kindling and started a fire while Shelby rummaged through the music CDs, selected one, and plugged it into the boom box. Classical stuff, baroque, a violin concerto—Vivaldi, he thought. She knew he didn't much care for that kind of thing; his taste in classical music ran to the soft background variety, Brahms or Mozart, but what he really liked was jazz, any style but preferably Ellington or Coltrane or Miles Davis. He wondered if she'd picked Vivaldi to irritate him. No, she wouldn't do that. She wasn't petty. Probably chose that CD because it matched her mood.

Shelby curled up with a book in one of the chairs facing the fire. So he rummaged around in the bookcase and found a local history of the

Mendocino coast from Gualala to Fort Bragg. History was a subject he'd always enjoyed—American, foreign, regional, all kinds. One of his pet peeves was the average person's ignorance of and disinterest in past events. How could you understand what was going on today in politics, economics, religion, countries like Iraq and Afghanistan, society in general if you didn't know or care what influenced and shaped each over years, decades, centuries? How could you support your opinions and make informed decisions without a historical foundation?

The book was easy reading and informative—a good thing, because his attention span wasn't what it used to be. He hadn't known that this part of the coast had been a hotbed of liquor smuggling during Prohibition. Ships loaded with Canadian whiskey had made regular runs down from British Columbia, anchoring just outside the five-mile limit, and rumrunners had gone out in launches and fishing boats and brought in cases and hid them in barns until they could be trucked inland across the Coast Range. Around the time of Repeal there'd been a gun battle between bootleggers and federal agents in a place called Bourne's Landing, near Gualala. One of the agents had been wounded and another one kidnapped and held hostage.

Exciting times. Bad times, too. Andrew Volstead's so-called noble experiment had been anything but. Hadn't somebody once said that the country would've been saved a lot of grief if Volstead had been a drunk like everybody else?

Macklin lowered the book so he could watch Shelby over the top of it, something he never tired of doing. Her slender body was as flexible as a cat's; she sat coiled with her legs tucked under her, her head tilted away from him, seemingly absorbed in her paperback. Her face, in profile and lit by the fire, had a kind of Madonna-like radiance.

He loved her so damn much.

TEN

ON THE ROAD AGAIN . . .
He liked driving the coast highway. Day or night, rain or shine, it
didn't really matter. He'd been here long enough, put in enough hours
traveling back and forth along the fifty-some miles between Jenner and
Fort Bragg, so that he knew every twist and turn and switchback. He could
drive Highway 1 in his sleep now if he felt like it. Not too fast, not too
slow, always with pleasure and always in control.

Always in control.

He liked being close to the ocean, too. He wished he'd been born and
raised with the Pacific in his backyard, or at least that he'd discovered it a
lot sooner than he had. He'd been to a lot of different places in his life
and there wasn't one even close to as good as this. He liked everything
about the area. In clear weather the eye-stinging silver sparkle of sunlight
on the water, and the way the moon glinted off its smooth blackness at
night. On wet days the clean smell of the rain and how the big waves
rolled up hard and glare-white against the shoreline. The sea wind in his
face, salt tang in his nostrils. The gulls and pelicans and other seabirds,
even the squawking crows that wheeled around overhead like miniature
stealth aircraft. The state and county parks, the wilderness areas, the coves
and gulches and beaches, the pastureland where sheep and cattle grazed,
the stands of old-growth pines and redwoods along the cliffs and inland
hills . . . all of it open and beautiful and unspoiled.

That was what mattered most to him, that this part of the coast was still largely unspoiled.

Oh, sure, there were people and wherever you had people, you had the trappings of what passed for civilization—trailer parks and campgrounds, motels and inns and B&Bs and restaurants and gift shops and minimalls. But they were widely scattered and for the most part they weren't offensive, they blended in—as Sea Ranch, the ten-mile stretch of retirement and rental homes south of Gualala, blended in—because the residents and the Coastal Commission demanded it. He didn't mind most of the people, either, the full-time or part-time residents and the visitors and pass-throughs who made an effort to maintain the area as God and nature intended. People like him who understood how important open space and natural beauty were in a world filled with ugliness. Brothers and sisters under the skin.

The handful who crapped it up, defiled the coast, defiled nature were the ones he hated, the ones he terminated . . . exterminated. Like those kids with their fast-food leavings strewn all over the pristine white sand down near Fort Ross. Like the motorcycle drunk throwing garbage at the sea lions and the clear-cutting old man and the abalone poacher. Exterminated was exactly the right word. Like taking out al-Qaida terrorists, or swatting mosquitoes and stepping on cockroaches. Ridding the world of polluters and vandals and spoilers was no different than ridding it of insurgents and disease-carrying vermin.

Society called it murder, but society wasn't always right. He didn't enjoy using his weapon, never had and never would. It didn't make him feel powerful or even particularly righteous. What it did do was give him a sense of accomplishment, of having done his small part for the common good—same as fighting a war. He'd never thought of himself as a nature lover or a protector of the environment until these past few months, but that was what he was—not one of those mealy-mouthed public figures who talked and talked and sucked around and compromised and never got anything done, but a man who bit the bullet and used the bullet to do what was necessary. Proactive. Wasn't that the word? A proactive soldier in the army of destruction of nature's enemies.

He went pleasure driving late that afternoon for the first time since Christmas. The holidays were no big deal to him, never had been. Even when he was with other people he felt cut off from Christmas and all the commercialized bullshit that went with it. It hadn't been too bad this year, though. Dealing with the poacher had made it into a celebration.

He didn't get behind the wheel today because he was looking for the enemy, a soldier on a search-and-destroy mission; he never went out with that specific objective in mind. The enemy was here, there, everywhere in the fifty-plus miles of coastline, small in number, sure, but they always stood out like targets on a firing range; he didn't need to go hunting to find one.

A lot of the scattered traffic on the highway was official, highway patrolmen and extra deputies from the county seat in Ukiah, and he took his time, not exactly poking along but keeping at or just below the speed limit. No reason for any of the officers to give him a second look, but still he had to be careful not to call attention to himself in any way.

Streamers from a dense offshore fog bank laid a misty sheen over the windshield, so he kept the wipers going. No problem. He liked the fog even when it slicked the road surface, got thick enough, as it was doing now, to hide some of the inlets and most of the ocean. He didn't even mind the storms, like the one yesterday, though he didn't do much pleasure driving when the wind and the rain got too heavy. Hazardous. Some drivers took chances no matter what the conditions; you just didn't know who might be out in rough weather, some idiot with a two-thousand-pound lethal weapon in his hands putting other folks' lives in jeopardy.

Nice and warm in the car, with the heater going. He had the radio going, too. You couldn't get much on it up here except a couple of local stations and the one out of Santa Rosa; the others on both AM and FM would tune in for a while, clear and sharp, and then fade out. The station he liked best played a mix of golden oldies, R&B, and country-western. Little bit of everything, and not much talk.

Another he liked sometimes when he was in the right mood was the religious station, but it was still playing Christmas music today, "O Little Town of Bethlehem" shot through with static when he tuned in. Carols he could do without, but he didn't mind old-fashioned gospel music now and then; and some of the Bible quotations and sermons were worth listening to and thinking about. But he couldn't stand the loudmouths who came on and started jabbering about politics and family values and gay marriage, telling you what God said was right and wrong and good and evil and what you should believe and how you should behave. That was why he didn't listen to the station very often. Besides, it was one of those that kept fading out.

One thing he avoided completely was local news broadcasts. He'd listened to one once, after those two kids down by Fort Ross, and he hadn't liked what they'd said about him. They didn't understand anything about his mission. Said he must be crazy, an off-the-rails vigilante playing God. Crap like that upset him because it didn't have a speck of truth. How could somebody who'd never met him, didn't have a clue about what went on inside his head, know what kind of man he was? Impossible. So why should he be subjected to their bullshit opinions?

Well, out of hearing, out of mind. Driving, now, that was something worth paying attention to.

As far as he was concerned, driving topped the list of life's enjoyments. It relaxed you, took your mind off things that bothered you, kept you focused. And when he drove the coast highway, he felt as though he were traveling back and forth along the edge of the world. Yet there was never any sense that he might drop off into nothingness. Just the opposite. He felt anchored for the first time in his life, as if he and the car were running on invisible tracks. As if he were safely locked in and yet totally free at the same time, and that if he wanted to he could drive along the edge of the world forever.

A vehicle going faster than he was came barreling up behind him, its headlights stabbing fuzzy-bright through the mist and gathering darkness. The lights closed in, steadied like huge yellow eyes in the rearview mirror. Tailgater. There were a lot of them on the highway, residents who'd driven it for years and knew the twists and turns better than he did, reckless kids and race-driver wannabes; but if this one had come flying up on a sheriff's cruiser or a highway patrol car, it would've bought him an unsafe-driving ticket damn quick.

Under the circumstances the safest thing for him to do was to pull over and let the idiot pass. But there was no place to do that here, on a twisty section hemmed in by trees on both sides. Increasing his speed slightly didn't get the other vehicle off his tail, either.

Half a mile of this, the constant crowding, started to piss him off. He thought about slowing down to twenty-five or so, making a challenge thing out of it, and he might have done that if the road hadn't straightened out as he came through a tight curve. Double yellow line, no passing, but that didn't stop the other driver; the glaring headlights swung out and around, the dark shape of a pickup roared by and then cut in in front of him, not quite close enough to force him to brake. One of the pickup's taillights was out; the other flashed like a bloody eye and then began to dwindle as the driver gathered speed.

His first impulse was to give chase, catch the bastard, force him off and confront him and then terminate him. But an impulse was all it was, intense for a few seconds, then overcome and gone. Giving in to road rage was foolish, dangerous. The pickup's driver had committed a stupid traffic crime, but that wasn't sufficient cause for him to take action. Crimes against nature were the only cause for him to use deadly force. Today, or at any time, ever. If he started eliminating individuals who were guilty of other crimes, that would make him just what society believed he was—an out-of-control avenger, a vigilante playing God.

He slowed down, relaxing again, recapturing the good feeling he'd had before the tailgater showed up. The radio was playing a Willie Nelson song, something about blue eyes crying in the rain. Not exactly cheerful, but he liked it anyway. He liked Willie's music. Mostly gentle, meaningful songs about love and loss, happiness and sadness, sin and redemption—genuine human emotions. Old Willie had a reputation for being an outlaw, but he really wasn't. Any more than he himself was an outlaw. That was something the two of them had in common—mislabeled outlaws.

The fog kept thickening, feelers of dark gray wrapping themselves around the pines. The way it was doing that reminded him of the Christ-mas trees his mother put up in their house when he was a kid, the same blue spruce with the same decorations every year. Tinsel . . . she loved that glittery silver tinsel. Garlands, too, white garlands. Silver and white woven through and around the thick-needled branches. And blue lights and blue ornaments, she never wanted any other color but blue.

Once, when he was nine or ten, he'd brushed against the tree acciden-tally and knocked off some tinsel and a blue sparkly bell, one of her fa-vorite ornaments, that shattered when it hit the floor, and she heard the noise and came running in and screamed at him, "You clumsy little shit. Why can't you watch where you're going? Well? What's the matter with you, standing there like that? Clean it up! How many times I got to tell you to clean up your messes?"

Bad memory. He didn't like thinking about his mother, long dead and gone and unmissed. Or any part of growing up in that hardscrabble West Texas town. He'd come a long way since he left when he was eighteen to join the army and he wasn't ever going back, not for any reason.

The highway straightened again into a long reach. Ahead on the sea-ward side, the land stretched out to a wide, flat-topped promontory like a fat handless arm reaching into the ocean; a ribbon of blacktop traced over to a parking area and lookout, and there was a sign at the intersection that said Scenic Point. He'd gone out there a couple of times. Nice view from the lookout; you could see the contours of the shoreline for quite a distance in both directions, and just offshore a massive hunk of shale shaped like the prow of a ship reared up out of the sea.

A car was parked on the lookout, facing seaward. Tourist taking in the view? Not too likely, this time of year and this late in the day. Somebody with car trouble, maybe. If that was it, he might be able to help. He braked and turned off onto the blacktop.

Low-slung sports car, he saw as he neared. Porsche, looked like. He didn't much care for cars like that, or the kind of people who drove them. Too fast and reckless, no regard for anybody else's safety, like that asshole tailgater. This one was black and had familiar lines, but there were a lot of them like this zooming up and down the coast highway.

His headlights washed over the other vehicle; the driver seemed to
be the only occupant. Sitting there quietly—looking, waiting? Or doing
something else, like swilling booze, getting ready to smash a bottle on the
asphalt or the rocks below or throw it at a sea creature like that drunken
motorcycle rider on the Navarro River?

Friend—or enemy?

He pulled up a few yards away, transferred the 9-mil Glock from the
glove compartment to his coat pocket, and went to find out.

ELEVEN

NIGHT.

A martini for Shelby and half a glass of wine for him while good jazz played soft in the background—Macklin's CD choice this time, Miles Davis's *Kind of Blue*. Crab salad, leftover sourdough, half a bottle of chardonnay. One of the DVDs from Ben's collection, his choice again—a farcical boy-meets-girl comedy that was watchable if not particularly funny. Quiet time again, more wood on the fire, the last of the wine from dinner in Shelby's glass.

The combination of heat and music and food had relaxed him for the first time in days. Again he watched the firelight play over the smooth contours of Shelby's face, the familiar curves of her body. Tenderness welled in him. And, inevitably, desire.

He said, "Remember that trip to Big Sur right after we were married? The cabin in the woods?"

"What made you think of that?"

"Sitting in front of the fire like this."

She was silent.

"That's not all we did in front of the fire," he said.

Still silent.

"There's plenty of room in front of this one, too. I could go get a blanket from the bedroom . . ."

"No," she said.

"Just like that? No?"

"Not tonight, Jay. I'm not in the mood."

One of the burning logs dropped off the grate, sending up a shower of sparks that glowed bright red before winking out; his desire died just as quickly. "Seems like you're not in the mood a lot lately. It didn't used to be like that—you used to be horny all the time."

"A lot of things used to be different." She stirred out of her chair. "I think I'll take a hot bath."

"You don't have to lock the door," he called after her. "I won't come in and try to wash your back."

Bed. Shelby turned away from him, the cold, rhythmic sound of the rain on the roof adding to his feeling of loneliness. Sleep was a long time coming.

And when it did—

Dark place, warm, safe. Sleeping.

Not sleeping anymore. Listening.

What're those noises? Loud, weird.

Thump. Grunt, slurp, screech, squeal. Thump thump thump.

Something's out there.

Something . . . terrible.

I have to find out what it is. But I don't want to. I'm afraid.

Squeal, howl, slurp. Thump thump thump thump thump.

Oh God, what if it tries to hurt me?

Stay here, don't move.

No, I can't, I have to find out what it is—

Dark place, cold. Walking.

Long tunnel, shadows crawling on the walls, faint glow from somewhere that lets me see where I'm going. The floor feels like it's made of ice, I start to shiver from the chill. Walking straight, turning right, walking straight, turning left—

Light ahead, so bright it hurts my eyes. The noises come from behind it—grunt, slurp, thump thump squeal thump. I want to stop walking toward the light, I'm afraid of what I'll see, but I have to find out what's making those sounds.

Closer. And into the light, through the light.

No! No!

Monster.

Horrible, hairy thing and what it's doing, what it's doing—

Slurp, thump, slurp slurp.

It's feeding!

I make a sound, I can't help myself, and the thing rises up from the carcass of whatever it's eating, its open mouth and yellow-spike teeth dripping crimson. It looks around at me, then lets loose an ear-splitting roar and leaps up with long sharp claws slicing the air and comes lurching toward me spitting fire.

Run! Hide!

And I run out of the light into the shadows, run through the tunnel, I've never run faster . . . but I can't run fast enough, the thing is close behind me, I feel its fire breath and hear the pounding click of its claws—

Dark place again, and I'm down on all fours crawling into another dark place. Trying to make myself smaller, squirming like a worm into a hole, hide, hide!

Too late.

The thing is there, looming over me, I see the awful twisted shape of it as it bends down and . . . oh Jesus it wraps a claw around my arm and yanks me upward. Pain erupts, then wild panic as it drags me close to its red drooling mouth.

It's going to eat me!

But first it shakes me, hard, my teeth rattle like bones, I smell the hot stink of its breath in my face. Spiraling terror makes me pee on myself. The thing roars again and shakes me harder, and then it—

—rips my arm off and hurls it on the floor—

—and rips my head off and hurls it on the floor—

—and my head rolls into the wall, wobbles and stops, and my eyes stare up, stare up—

—and I'm looking at my wriggling mutilated body wet all over with piss and blood—

—and the creature's mouth opens wider, yawning like a cavern, and from the floor I hear it booming out words in a voice loud as thunder but I can't understand them, the words somehow fall like whispers against my ears—

—and in horror I watch my headless body being stuffed inside its gaping mouth—

—and then the yellow spikes gnash down and the chewing starts, and I scream and scream and scream—

Macklin was awake now, shaky and bathed in sweat, his breath coming in short grinding gasps. Another nightmare ride, the same every time in every detail, ending when the imaginary monster begins to eat his headless body and he screams himself out of it. Shelby was alert beside him in the dark bedroom, trying with hands and words to calm him. He heard himself say, "I'm all right, I'm all right," but he wasn't. His heart felt as if it would burst. One of these times it just might.

She said, "Lie still, shallow breaths," and got out of bed and hurried into the bathroom.

He lay still, willing his pulse rate to slow. He'd been having the nightmare for so long he couldn't remember when it first started. Until his life had degenerated into the string of failures, he'd gone as long as two years without a replay; since Conray terminated him it came more frequently. He didn't understand it, didn't have a clue what it meant or what triggered it. Some deep-rooted fear . . . the fear of death? He just didn't know.

Shelby came out with a wet towel, sponged the sweat off his face. Better now, with the towel draped across his forehead. The tightness still felt like a closed hand inside his chest, but the blood-pound in his ears had lessened and he was breathing more easily. He'd be okay.

Until the next time.

She said, "It might help if you'd tell me about it."

He couldn't. He'd never told anyone. A kid's fantasy monster nightmare . . . stupid, too embarrassing to talk about. But real—so bloody *real*.

"No, it wouldn't," he said. "Don't keep asking me, okay?"

It was an hour or more before he slept again.

TWELVE

ANOTHER GRAY, GLOOMY, WINDY day. The rear deck, the grassy slope, and the side patio were all wet with dew. Shelby stepped outside for a few seconds to see how cold it was. *Damn* cold—the wind slapped at her face like a frostbitten hand, the sharp smell of ozone pinched her nostrils. There'd be more rain pretty soon, probably another storm.

The cold and damp were in the cottage, too. Jay had turned on the baseboard heater when he got up and it had been going for half an hour now, but the moist chill was still in the air. How could that happen overnight in a place as well built as this one? One of the joys of oceanfront living in the dead of winter, she thought. Goose bumps and sniffles to go with the whitewater views and invigorating sea breezes.

The place was already beginning to give her cabin fever.

Jay made buttermilk pancakes for breakfast, his special recipe that included bananas and nutmeg and some other kind of spice. They were good but she only picked at the ones on her plate; she didn't have much appetite. For the food or for the conversation he tried to make. Small talk as usual. Not a word about the nightmare, or about anything else that mattered to either of them.

Finally she said, "I don't think I can just sit around here another day. Let's go for a drive."

"Where?"

"I don't know. Fort Bragg's not far, is it?"

"Twenty miles or so."

"You sound hesitant."

"No, it's just that . . ."

"Just that what?"

"There's another storm coming," he said.

"Surprise."

"No, I mean a big storm, worse than the one on the way up. High winds, heavy rain."

"How do you know? The car radio?"

"The woman in the Seacrest grocery store."

"And you didn't tell me until now?"

"I guess I just forgot."

You guess you just forgot. Bullshit, Jay.

She said, "When is this big storm supposed to get here?"

"Sometime this afternoon."

"Then there's still time for a drive to Fort Bragg."

"If you really want to go."

"I really want to go."

"Okay, then." He reached across to touch her hand; she resisted an impulse to pull it away. "We'll leave right after I clean up."

"Cleaning up can wait until we get back. I'll do it. You don't always have to be maid as well as cook."

"Just trying to make things a little easier for you."

Five minutes later they were in the car. She felt better being out of the cottage, moving again. The highway to the north was full of loops and twists, but she had to admit the scenery was impressive. Ocean views, wooded areas, a long sweep around the mouth of a river, hamlets and rustic inns and B&Bs. Wind gusts buffeted the car and the sky was a sullen chiaroscuro, but the windshield stayed dry.

Jay kept trying to make conversation, but it was all small talk and she was sick of small talk. They were passing by the picturesque bluff-top town of Mendocino when he said something about it looking so much like villages in Maine, the producers of the TV show *Murder, She Wrote* had passed it off as Cabot Cove for the duration of the series. More small talk, trivial and meaningless.

Enough, she thought.

"Jay," she said, "talk to me."

"I am talking to you. I said—"

"You didn't *say* anything. You haven't said anything I really wanted to hear in so long I can't remember the last time."

She saw the muscles along his jaw clench. "That's not fair, Shel."

"Fair? My God, *fair*?"

"What do you want me to say?"

"What you're thinking, what you're feeling."

"You know how I feel about you. I love you."

"That's not what I mean and you know it. Half the time you talk to me as if I'm a casual acquaintance instead of your wife. Never about anything that really matters to you. Stop hiding from me."

"I'm not hiding from you," he said, "I'm . . . I can't always express what I'm thinking or feeling . . ."

"Can't or won't?"

"It's hard, that's all. I'm just not wired the way you are, I'm . . . I have this . . . oh Jesus, do we *have* to get into this now?"

"If not now, then when?"

"When we're back home. There're some things . . . I'll tell you then."

"Why can't you tell me now?"

"I just . . . I don't want to spoil our last couple of days up here."

"Spoil them by clearing the air?"

"When we get home—that's a promise."

"Another promise you won't keep. You'll go right on hiding in that private cocoon of yours."

"No, I won't. Not this time."

Useless. Like beating her head against a stone wall.

The fantasy came over her again. He seemed to waver in her vision, turn shimmery, lose definition; for a second or two it was as if she could look right through him. The illusion was almost frightening this time.

She closed her eyes to shut it out, shifted over close against the door and laid her head against the seat back. The silence that rebuilt between them was like a weight. A frustrated anger simmered in her, but it didn't last. In its place was a small, cold emptiness.

And she thought again: Enough.

THIRTEEN

M ACKLIN'S MOOD MATCHED THE sullen, cloud-heavy morning as they approached Fort Bragg. Little confrontational scenes like the one he'd just had with Shelby always left him feeling depressed. Powerless, too. Not against her, but against himself and the intractable compulsion to hold back. She didn't ask much of him, and the one important thing she did ask he seemed incapable of giving her. It made him dislike himself all the more.

Scared him all the more.

The thought of what lay ahead fretted him again, brought that closed-fist feeling back into his chest. The coming year would likely make the last few seem happy by comparison. He was pretty sure he knew how Shelby would take the news and just what she'd say, the same thing she'd said at the other crisis points in their life together: "We'll get through it." But would they this time? He didn't see how it was possible, not in the long run. This was so much harder to take than the other setbacks, ongoing and irreversible.

The prospect of life without her scared the hell out of him. Barren. Lonely. Yet even if she was willing to put up with him over the long haul, he wasn't willing to become any more of a burden to her than he already was. If the situation grew unbearable, as it was liable to pretty quickly, he'd be the one to do the walking. He'd promised himself that and he wouldn't renege. His gift to her, the best gift he could ever give her—her freedom.

He didn't know where he'd go or what he'd do if it came to that. Except to get the hell out of Cupertino, put as much distance between them as he could. Head for Tucson, maybe. Tom would take him in, at least for a while; they weren't close anymore, but his younger brother was a strong believer in family values, family support. But Tom and Jenna had three kids and a mortgage and bills to pay—they couldn't afford to shelter him for long, even if he could find some kind of work to pay for temporary room and board. He'd be a burden on them, and he couldn't allow that to happen either. Better to spare Tom and his family and not go to Tucson at all.

What, then? Crawl into a warm little private hole somewhere? He'd be able to manage alone if circumstances allowed him to earn a living wage, but the one thing he'd never do was to go on welfare. If things got that bad, if there was no longer any hope and he was of no use to himself or anyone else, he'd take himself out. There were ways, painless ways, and he'd done enough soul-searching to know that he was capable of it.

Quality of life. A phrase people used a lot nowadays, one that was absolutely true. No quality, no point to living. Simple as that.

They were in Fort Bragg now, crossing a long bridge that spanned the entrance to the harbor. Small seaside town, population seven or eight thousand, that had once been the home base for Georgia Pacific, the largest lumber mill on the north coast; now it was the fishing industry and tourism that supported it. There wasn't much of either this time of year. Under that dark, threatening sky it, too, had a bleak aspect that an array of lighted holiday decorations failed to alleviate.

Beneath the bridge and along the harborfront to the east there was a collection of restaurants, fish shops, and docks for commercial fishing boats and whale-watching and sportfishing charters. Shelby had no interest in the town or in stopping for lunch—she spoke to him in short, clipped sentences, when she spoke at all—but he drove down to the harbor anyway. Her favorite fish was wild salmon; he thought maybe a couple of fresh sockeye filets for dinner would put her in a better mood. Pathetic peace offering, but he didn't have any other kind to make.

She waited in the car while he went into one of the fish shops. Just as well, because there was a newspaper rack in front and the Santa Rosa paper's front-page headline jumped out at him as he went by.

SEARCH FOR COASTLINE KILLER INTENSIFIES

Long, silent ride back down Highway 1. Macklin didn't even try to make conversation. The rain continued to hold off, but by the time they passed the mouth of the Navarro River the wind gusts were fierce and there was more black than gray in the cloud churn overhead. It wouldn't be long before the skies opened up and the rain spilled out.

Coming from the north, he missed the Ocean Point Lane intersection and had to turn around and retrace a quarter of a mile. Mr. Inept. The first drops of rain from the bloated cloud bellies had begun to speckle the windshield as he drove through the jog in the road past the big estate. At almost the same instant he saw the vehicles parked in front of the Lomax house.

"Now what the hell's going on?"

Shelby stirred beside him. "What?"

"Up there. Look."

Macklin put on the wipers to clear away the rain mist. Shelby still had to lean forward, squinting, because of the sticking blade on her side. There were two cars, a dark-colored sedan angled into the entrance driveway and a sheriff's department cruiser on the blacktop.

"You don't suppose Lomax really hurt her this time?" he said. "Bad enough to put her in the hospital?"

Shelby's jaw tightened; she shook her head.

"Or maybe she did something to him. If it's bad, I hope that's the way it was."

"It may not be anything at all."

Instead of turning into the cottage's drive, he rolled on past fifty yards or so—close enough to make out a seal on the driver's door of the parked sedan. Highway patrol.

"Two official cars parked out there like that," he said. "It's sure not a social visit."

"Not an emergency, either. No flashing lights and I don't see an ambulance."

"Could be parked inside the fence. Or it hasn't gotten here yet."

She said, to herself as much as to him, "I wish I knew what happened."

"Well, we can't go up and ask. We'll probably never know."

FOURTEEN

They had been in the cottage less than fifteen minutes and Jay was making noises about going out to the lane "to see if the law's still up there" when the doorbell chimed. He glanced at Shelby, muttered, "What the hell?" and went to open the door on its chain lock.

She saw him stiffen slightly as he looked out. "Yes, what is it?" The quickened beat of the wind blurred the voice outside, but whatever it said convinced him to remove the chain and pull the door wide. Two men came inside, one wearing an unbuttoned overcoat over a suit and tie, the other in a deputy sheriff's uniform. Both wore grim, tight-lipped expressions. The man in the overcoat saw Shelby, approached her with a leather ID case open in his hand.

"Mrs. Macklin?"

"Hunter," she said automatically, looking at the badge inside the case. "Shelby Hunter."

"I understood you and Mr. Macklin were married."

"We are. I kept my birth name."

"Oh, I see. Well." He put the ID case away. "My name is Rhiannon, Lieutenant George Rhiannon. I'm an investigator with the highway patrol. This is Deputy Randall Ferguson, county sheriff's department."

She nodded. Jay's eyes were on the deputy—a big, youngish man with a bristly mustache and flat green eyes, standing in a ruler-backed posture like a soldier at attention.

"You're the officer who led us out here the other night," he said.

"That's right."

"Well . . . what can we do for you?"

"We won't take up much of your time," Rhiannon said. "Just a few questions, if you don't mind." He was in his forties, with an ovoid body on short stubby legs and a dark, pointy, long-nosed face. Like a dachshund that had acquired human features and learned how to walk on its hind legs, Shelby thought. But there was nothing comical about the man or his demeanor. His movements, his words had a sharp professional economy.

"What's happened?" she asked.

"I understand you spent some time with your neighbors and their houseguests Sunday night."

"Just long enough to have a drink with them. We went there to borrow matches when the power went out."

"Everything seem to be all right with the four of them?"

"They'd been drinking pretty heavily," Jay said. "We picked up on a lot of tension."

"Any specific cause?"

"Not that we could tell."

"Conflict between Eugene Decker and anyone in the party?"

"His wife. They were at each other's throats."

"Between Decker and the Lomaxes?"

"There was some sniping. None of them were getting along."

"Have you seen Mr. Decker since then?"

"No."

"Any of the others?"

"Mrs. Decker. Yesterday morning, at the store in Seacrest. She was on her way home to Santa Rosa."

"Did you talk to her?"

"Briefly."

"She tell you why she was leaving, going home?"

Jay related the gist of the conversation.

"Any other contact with any of the four since Monday?" Rhiannon asked.

Shelby said, "I saw Mrs. Lomax—Claire. On the beach yesterday morning. We had a brief conversation."

"About what?"

"Is that important?"

"She has some facial injuries," Rhiannon said. "She have them then?"

"Yes."

"Tell you how she got them?"

What Claire had told her had been in confidence; Rhiannon hadn't given a reason for her to break it. "It wasn't any of my business."

"She told us she tripped and fell and her husband backs her up. But it looks more like an assault. What do you think?"

"Is she all right now?"

"No further injuries, if that's what you mean. You haven't answered my question, Mrs., ah, Hunter."

"It doesn't matter what I think, does it?"

"What's going on?" Jay said. "If Lomax and his wife are both okay, how come you're here? Did one of them call you?"

"No, sir."

"Decker, then?"

Ferguson said, "He can't call anyone. He's dead."

Shelby blinked her surprise. Jay said, "Dead?"

"Found in his Porsche down the coast this morning."

"An accident?"

"No, not an accident."

"Natural causes?"

"He was shot through the head."

". . . My God. The Coastline Killer?"

"Looks that way."

Rhiannon gave the deputy a sharp look before he said to Jay, "We don't know anything for sure right now."

"Except that it wasn't suicide," Ferguson said. "No weapon in the car."

Shelby's throat felt clogged, as if she'd swallowed something small and hard that wouldn't go down. "Coastline Killer? Who's that?"

"You don't know?"

"No. I don't."

"Funny. Your husband seems to. Ask him."

Jay wouldn't look at her. He said to Rhiannon, "When was Decker killed?"

"Sometime yesterday. According to the Lomaxes, he decided to go on home himself and left sometime in the afternoon."

"They tried to talk him out of it because he'd been drinking," Ferguson said. "He should've listened to them." The deputy had begun to move around the front room, looking here and there as if he were checking out a crime scene. "Were you here yesterday afternoon, Mr. Macklin?"

"Yes."

"All afternoon?"

"Yes, all afternoon. Why?"

"We're trying to determine the exact time Mr. Decker left," Rhiannon said. "Neither of the Lomaxes is certain."

"Well, I can give you a pretty good idea. We were coming up from the beach when we heard him drive by out front. It was a little before two thirty."

"You're sure about the time?"

"Sure enough. I glanced at my watch just after we came inside. Two thirty on the nose then."

Rhiannon scribbled in his notebook, closed it, and slid it into his overcoat pocket. "I think that's about all, then. Thanks for your cooperation."

Ferguson said, "You folks wouldn't be planning to leave right away, would you?"

"No. Not until New Year's Day."

"Are you going to want to talk to us again?" Shelby asked.

Rhiannon said he doubted that would be necessary.

Ferguson was still looking at Jay. "Reason I asked, there's a bad storm coming—worse than the one Sunday. Once it hits, the highway's liable to be pretty hazardous for the next twenty-four hours or so. Be a good idea for you to stay here until it blows through."

"We'll do that," Jay said. "Right here."

When the two men were gone, he put the chain back on the door and threw the bolt lock. He said then, "I don't like that deputy. Did you see the way he kept looking at me with those funny eyes of his?"

Shelby kept still.

"Suspicious, just like the other night. What the hell reason does he have for being suspicious of me?"

She didn't respond to that, either.

"Lomax, yes, sure. One look at Claire's face and they had to know what kind of bastard he is. Make any cop suspicious. But people like us—"

"Quit trying to avoid the issue, Jay," she said. "Who the hell is the Coastline Killer?"

His expression changed. "Ah, God," he said.

"Who, dammit?"

For a few seconds she thought he wasn't going to answer. Then, as if the words were being dragged out of him, "Some lunatic who's been shooting people along the coast over the past several months. They don't have any idea who or why."

"Shooting people. How many people?"

"Five now, maybe more."

Five, maybe more. Lord!

"Where along the coast?"

"Different places," he said. "The first ones . . . those two kids in sleeping bags, down by Fort Ross, remember? Picks his victims at random."

"And the latest was Gene Decker."

"You never think it can happen to somebody you know, even slightly, somebody so nearby . . . Christ, it gives you the willies. Poor bastard must've been in the wrong place at the wrong time." Talking too fast, almost jabbering. Still not meeting her eyes. "I wonder how Paula's taking it. Fed up with him playing around, thinking about a divorce, but still—"

Shelby said, "How long have you known about this Coastline Killer? Since before we left home?"

"No," he said. "Only since yesterday, from the man at the service station in Seacrest."

"And you 'forgot' to tell me, like you 'forgot' about the storm."

"I didn't see how it could have any effect on us. None of the shootings was in this immediate area—" Another headshake, then a small, empty gesture. "I'm sorry, I know I should've told you."

"I don't want to hear that," she said.

"I really am sorry—"

"I said I don't want to hear it."

She went over and sat down at the dinette table. Outside the wind whistled and cried and rain thrummed on the roof, ticked against the seaward walls and windows like handfuls of flung pellets. Water streaked and ran on the window glass; everything out there had a smeared, indistinct appearance, like faulty underwater photography.

"I'd better go bring in some more wood," Jay said, "before the weather gets any worse."

She didn't answer.

He went away and a little while later he came back. He said something to her, but she didn't listen to it. The rain and wind sounds seemed magnified now, as if they'd somehow gotten inside her head. It wasn't until he said her name, sharply, that she lifted her head to look at him. And when she did, it was as if he wasn't even there, as if he had finally and completely disappeared.

"Shel? Are you all right?"

"I want a divorce," she said.

FIFTEEN

*D*ARK PLACE, WARM, SAFE. *Sleeping.*
Not sleeping anymore. Listening.
What're those noises? Loud, weird.
Thump. Grunt, slurp, screech, squeal. Thump thump thump.
Something's out there.
Something . . . terrible.
I have to find out what it is. But I don't want to. I'm afraid.
Squeal, howl, slurp. Thump thump thump thump thump.
Oh God, what if it tries to hurt me?
Stay here, don't move.
No, I can't, I have to find out what it is . . .

. . . And he was through it and out of it, sweating, struggling for air. Disoriented at first—he didn't know where he was. Not in bed; the surface under him was cold, leathery, and Shelby wasn't beside him. Moment of panic, and then he was awake enough to remember that he'd sacked out on the living room couch under a blanket. "I don't want to sleep with you tonight," she'd said, and he hadn't argued, let her have the main bedroom. He could have slept in the guest room but it was too cold back there. Cold out here now, too, nothing left of the fire but a collection of ashes and dying embers.

The dream images were still vivid. The same, always the same. And yet there was something just a little different about this one . . . the creature's snarling, howling words at the end, that were somehow like whispers so he couldn't make them out. This time they'd seemed louder, almost but not quite understandable. Ugly, terrifying words he never wanted to hear . . . except that at a deeper level of perception, he did because he sensed they might explain the nightmare.

He rubbed sweat off his face with a corner of the blanket, listening to the runaway pumping of his heart. It stuttered every few beats and his breathing came short and hot in his chest. One sudden savage burst of pain and it would be all over for him, no more confrontations with his night monster, no more bitter defeats, just blackness and peace. But it didn't happen. The thudding slowed, the sensation of gripping tightness eased, his respiration gradually slowed to near normal.

They were coming more often now, the nightmare rides. Two in two nights, the first time that had ever happened. Stress-induced. Or maybe there was some sort of physiological link. He had no control over them in any case, no way to put a stop to them. Ironic in a bitter, devilish way. Asleep, in the dream, he was at the mercy of a hideous being that ripped him apart and devoured him; awake, he was at the mercy of other demons beyond his control, real ones like failure and decay, that were in literal ways ripping him apart and devouring him.

A sudden blast of wind shook the cottage, rattled the windows in their frames. It had been storming heavily when he drifted off to sleep, but the storm seemed even worse now—elemental fury out there. The rain was torrential, making a steady jackhammer sound on the roof. Wind drafts in the chimney swirled up ashes and thin sparks and blew them out across the hearth. The night seemed alive with shrieks, whistles, fluttery moans.

The sweat on him had dried and even under the blanket he was shivery cold. When he was sure his legs would support him, he got up slowly and made his way to the draped windows. The baseboard heater under them made ticking sounds when he turned it up full. So the power was still on, something of a surprise given the way the storm was raging. But it would go out sooner or later. Damn well be sure of that.

Back on the couch, huddled under the blanket. And the brief scene from yesterday afternoon, when he'd come back inside with the load of wood, replayed again in his memory.

"I want a divorce."

". . . Jesus, you don't mean that."

"I do mean it. I can't live like this anymore."

"Like what?"

"Like strangers. You keeping things from me, hiding from me. Two people can't live together without communicating."

"Swear to God, it's not intentional. I don't mean to shut you out—"

"But you do. Sins of omission, Jay."

"I love you, you know that—"

"It's not enough! Once, yes, but not anymore. There's just too much distance between us. And I don't see any way to bring us back together."

He'd tried to tell her then, to rip that one glued down page right out of the Macklin book. The words were all there, a huge glob of them in his throat, choking him. He'd hacked up some of them, a disjointed, fumbling few, but it was too late, he'd waited too long. She didn't want to listen; clapped her hands over her ears and got up and walked out of the room.

If he'd gone after her, tried again . . . but he hadn't. Too late. Nothing he said now would change her mind.

She was dead serious about the divorce, the way she'd acted the rest of the day proved that. Avoiding him for the most part—reading in the bedroom or staring out the oceanfront windows or into the fire while Vivaldi or, worse, Saint-Saëns throbbed gloomily out of the boom box, not answering or responding in monosyllables when he spoke to her. Drinking too much, eating nothing. And then saying in a flat, distant voice that she didn't want to sleep with him and going to bed early, shutting the bedroom door after her, maybe locking it for all he knew.

He kept telling himself to talk to her anyway, get it all said—keeping everything bottled up at a crisis point like this was senseless, self-destructive, an indication of some sort of dementia. Telling himself it might, it just might, make a difference after all. But he didn't believe it. The feeling of hopelessness was oppressively strong.

Maybe part of it was the environment here, the close confines of the cottage, the nasty weather. Maybe the familiar atmosphere at home would make it easier to talk, give him a chance to change her mind.

He didn't believe that, either.

He'd already lost her. Just as he'd lost baseball and the ability to have children and Macklin's Grotto and the Conray job and everything else that mattered in his life. It didn't make any difference anymore whether or not he got past this lunatic compulsion to keep things locked up inside. Too late. When she'd said, "I want a divorce," it had been the marriage's death knell.

Shelby stayed in the bedroom most of the morning—sleeping, or maybe just avoiding him. How did she feel after yesterday? Happy, sad, relieved? Or as depressed as he was?

He drank two cups of strong black coffee, forced himself to swallow half a glass of grapefruit juice and part of a container of yogurt. Washed and dried the dishes. Tidied up the front room, using the fireplace brush to clean ashes and soot and flecks of bark off the hearthstones. *You don't have to be maid as well as cook.* The hell he didn't. What else had he been good for the past six months? What else was he good for now?

Wrapped in his raincoat, he made a couple of struggling trips through the gale to replenish the firewood supply. The storm was already among the worst he'd encountered; the wind gusts must be forty or fifty miles per hour, shaking the cottage like a dog shakes a bone, bending the trees low to the ground and sending twigs and needles and small torn branches skittering across the lawn and side patio. The rain was like a whipping bead curtain, thick strands of it blown inland at an undulant slant that was almost horizontal. Huge waves lashed the shoreline, gouting up clouds of white; the ocean's surface was like foam-flecked water boiling in a cauldron.

When he came in with the second carrier of firewood, Shelby was in the kitchen pouring a cup of coffee. Still in her bathrobe, hair uncombed, her face pinched and baggy-eyed. She hadn't slept any better than he had.

He said tentatively, "I can make you some breakfast."

"No, thanks. I'm not hungry."

"You should eat something . . ."

"Later."

He'd left the drapes closed over the windows; Shelby opened them, then folded herself into one of the facing chairs and stared out at the rain-distorted view.

Tell her, he thought as he unloaded the carrier into the wood box. Go ahead, do it now. But it was a dull thought, without resolve. The sense of fatalism overwhelmed him again and he said nothing. It was as if he were trying to fight his way out of restraints, a goddamn mental straightjacket that had his will bound and helpless.

Long day ahead. Long, long day.

At one thirty the power went out.

They knew it immediately because Shelby had switched on the floor lamp next to her chair. As soon as the bulb went dark, she said, "Perfect. Just perfect." The baseboard heater made one last pinging noise, like a death rattle. "Perfect," she said again, and stood to close the drapes while Macklin got a fire going.

Shelby poured her first glass of wine a little after two o'clock. Sure sign of how troubled she was; she seldom started drinking so early in the day. But he didn't say anything to her about it. There was nothing to say and even if there had been, it wouldn't have made any difference. She hadn't spoken to him since the power outage; it was as if he weren't even there.

Misery loves company. Where had he heard that recently? Oh, right, from Paula Decker on Sunday night. Well, it was bullshit. Misery didn't love company; misery wanted to be alone, curled up in some dark corner with a blanket over its head.

Paula Decker. And Gene Decker, suddenly dead, another victim of the Coastline Killer. He'd never known a victim of violence before, random or otherwise. Only met the wine salesman once and hadn't liked him, but still a human being he'd had brief contact with just a few nights ago. Nobody deserved to die the way Decker had, with a psycho's bullet in his brain. Frightening and unsettling, when that kind of random lunacy touched your life like this.

He wondered again how Paula was taking the news. It couldn't be an easy thing to deal with, no matter how she'd felt about her husband. As bad as things were for Shelby and him right now, Paula was a lot worse off. Claire Lomax, too. Always somebody worse off than you are.

Yeah, he thought, but you don't have to live their lives. The only life you have to live, the only visceral misery you have to face, is your own.

Three o'clock.

The storm was massive now, roaring and rampaging like the dream creature, assaulting everything in its path. Hurricanes were unheard of on the California coast, but this was what Macklin imagined the beginnings of one must be like. They were probably safe enough forted up in here, but there was no certainty of it; when one of the stronger wind gusts slammed into the cottage, the walls and windows shimmied from the impact.

As early as it was, most of the daylight was already gone. A thin puddinglike gloom had settled around them, relieved somewhat by the firelight and the rows of candles Shelby had set out. But all the flames flickered and wobbled, creating restive shadows; both cold air and dampness had seeped in past the weatherstripping on windows and doors and lingered despite the fire's heat. The atmosphere was oppressive. As if he and Shelby were the only two silent mourners in a storm-battered funeral home.

He said, "I can't stand listening to that much longer. How about putting some music on?"

"Let's see if we can get a news broadcast first."

She switched on the boom box, fiddled with the radio dials. Static, mostly, on the AM and FM stations. She managed to tune in a local station whose announcer was giving a storm report, something about a bad slide that had closed Highway 1 near Anchor Bay, but it broke up into static after half a minute or so. Briefly she switched over to the police band. More storm-related chatter—road blockages, a traffic accident in Point Arena. Nothing about the Coastline Killer. Why would there be? Even a psycho wasn't demented enough to go out looking for people to shoot on a night like this.

Shelby said, "Find a CD you want to listen to," and headed to the kitchen for a wine refill. Macklin stood up, thinking he might as well join her—self-defense, to take the raw edge off his nerves—and that was when he heard the sudden boomlike cracking sound.

It came from outside during a brief lull in the wind squalls, loud enough to override the tempest. His first thought was a thunderclap. But no, it had been different—

In the next second there was another blast of sound, this one of a crashing collision that shook the floor, rattled the furniture.

"My God," Shelby said from the kitchen, "that felt like an earthquake."

"Couldn't have been. No shaking."

"Close, whatever it was. Somewhere out front."

"I'd better go have a look," he said. "You stay here—no use both of us getting wet."

He hurried to the utility porch, dragged his raincoat off the hook, shrugged into it; pulled on his waterproof gloves and jammed the rain hat down over his head. Then he grabbed the flashlight, just in case; unlocked the door and opened it just far enough to squeeze his body through.

Out on the patio the banshee wind almost bowled him over as he struggled ahead to the gate. A rain-laden gust ripped it out of his hand, hurled it against the dripping shrubbery on the other side. He staggered through and down the drive onto the lane.

The blacktop's surface was littered with needles, cones, boughs, bare limbs; a runnel as wide as a small stream paralleled it on the inland side.

Macklin swung the flash beam left, then right, slatting rain out of his eyes. Dimly, then, through the sodden half-daylight, he saw what had happened, what lay some fifty yards ahead to the south. He took half a dozen faltering steps in that direction before he stopped and stood bent and staring, his jaw clenched so tightly small shoots of pain radiated up both sides of his face.

Down tree. Big one aslant across the lane, blocking it just beyond where the Coulter property joined that of the neighboring estate.

Macklin pushed ahead for a closer look, stopping again within a few yards of the fallen tree—a dead bull pine from the woods on the inland side, its trunk encased in some sort of parasitic vine, its upthrust branches bare except for rows of decaying cones. Vine leaves, loose cones, snapped-off limbs littered the lane and the soggy ground along its length. The upper branches had collapsed a section of the estate's border fence; the lower end of the splintered trunk was half-hidden among the standing pines, cracks in the asphalt radiating out from under its middle section. The lane was completely blocked. It didn't look like you could even walk around the damn thing on either side, you'd have to climb over it.

He'd seen enough. He battled the wind back to the cottage, pushed his way inside, shouldered the door shut behind him. Shelby was waiting next to the dinette table.

She said, "What was it? A falling tree?"

"Yeah. Across the lane near the end of the property."

"You mean we can't get out?"

"No way to drive around it on either side. I'll see if I can get through to emergency road service on my cell."

"Don't bother. I tried mine Monday morning—no signal."

He tried anyway. Nothing. Dead.

Shelby said, "Is there any way to push the tree off with the car?"

"Doubt it, too big and heavy."

"With two cars? I think that SUV we saw belongs to the Lomaxes."

"Maybe." But he didn't believe it. The pine bole was thick and the splintered end had looked to be wedged between the trunks of the pines surrounding it. "There's a better way. If Ben has a gas-powered chain saw, we ought to be able to cut through the upper end once the storm passes."

"Maybe in that locked shed behind the carport."

"I'll go see. There's a bunch of keys on a hook in the kitchen—one of them ought to open the padlock."

He took the keys and the flashlight out into the thick, ropy downpour. Stood hunched in front of the shed door, the flash tucked under his arm with the beam steady on the padlock. Among the keys were two small ones; the second fit the lock. But the staple was rusty and it took him a minute to free it from the case. He shined the light inside the shed.

Gardening tools—pick, shovel, rakes, trowels. Dull-bladed ax that a lumberjack wouldn't be able to wield effectively. Electric weed-whacker. Hedge clippers, a long-handled tree saw. Handsaws, hammers, and other small tools. A wheelbarrow, a push broom, a pile of roofing shingles, a clutter of useless odds and ends. Everything you needed for the maintenance of a cottage like this except a chain saw and the gas necessary to run it.

He closed up the shed, leaving the padlock hanging unclosed through the hasp, and struggled back to the cottage. "No chain saw," he told Shelby.

"Lomax is a builder. He's liable to have one."

"Yeah."

"He'll have to be told in any case. They wouldn't have heard or felt the tree come down—they're too far away."

"Might as well do it right now, while there's still some daylight left."

"You want me to go? You've been out twice already—"

"No, I'll do it. I'm already soaked."

Out into the blow for the third time, running bent to the carport. All he'd need now was for the car not to start . . . but that didn't happen, the engine caught on the first turn of the key. He backed out onto the lane, got the Prius turned and moving—toward the fallen tree first, to see if there was any chance of moving it alone.

The wind slammed into the car with enough force to rock it from side to side; he had to take a tension grip on the wheel to hold it steady. The wipers, on high speed but with the one blade still sticking, were barely able to keep the windshield clear of sluicing rainwater. He hunched forward with his nose only a few inches from the glass and his eyes slitted; it was the only way he could follow the jittery path of the headlights.

When he neared the tree, he eased off to the right—letting the high beams pick out a place where he could nose up against it. If there was any chance of moving it, it would have to be at the slender upper end.

No chance at all. The blacktop was too slippery and cone-littered, the trunk too thick and its base too tightly wedged. The Prius's rear tires couldn't gain traction, spun futilely; the pine didn't budge an inch.

Macklin jammed the gearshift into reverse, backed carefully to the cottage drive; turned and headed the other way.

House lights swam up out of the liquidy dusk; the Lomaxes' auxiliary generator was still working. But as he neared the entrance drive, Macklin saw that the gates across it were closed. He braked alongside, left the engine running as he got out.

The gates, their stanchions anchored into socket holes in the blacktop, weren't just closed, they were also chained and padlocked together. He caught hold of the two halves, shook and stretched them apart with enough force to rattle the chain. That created a gap between them, but it was too narrow for him to fit through.

He peered through the opening. No outside lights, no interior lights visible in the front part of the house. The ones he'd seen from down the lane filtered out from the living room at the rear. The bulky shape of the SUV loomed dark and dripping on the parking area.

He switched the flashlight on, aiming the ray at the front door of the house. It wasn't powerful enough to penetrate the downpour, and there was still enough daylight left to dilute the beam, but if either of the Lomaxes looked out this way they ought to be able to see it. He waggled the flash from side to side, up and down. Kept doing that for more than a minute, without getting any kind of response.

Finally he gave it up, slid back into the Prius and swiped trickling rivulets out of his eyes and off his face. It took him three tries to position the car so that it was facing the gates. They were made of solid wood, but the high-beam glare penetrated the gap between the two halves and shone glistening off the curtain of rain. He flicked the lights on and off, on and off, a dozen times.

That didn't get him anywhere, either. Even if Lomax noticed the signaling, he wasn't coming out.

In frustration he leaned hard on the horn. More wasted effort; they wouldn't be able to hear it through the wind shrieks and the ocean's roar. He pounded the wheel with his fist. He was wet, cold, wired up as taut as a guitar string. And his breathing was off a little, coming short and painful, the same as in the aftermath of one of the nightmares; he hadn't noticed it until now.

The hell with it. Tomorrow was soon enough to tell Lomax about the blocked lane, find out if he had a chain saw. None of them was going anywhere until then anyway.

SIXTEEN

THREE OF THE CANDLE flames had been snuffed by the incoming blast of wind when Jay shoved his way through the door. Shelby got the box of matches, relit the wicks. Still murky in there, like the gloom in an underground grotto, and it wasn't even full dark outside yet; shadows and clots of blackness seemed to lurk beyond the edges of light from the candles and the fire. She was feeling the old fear of dark, empty places again. It never bothered her when she worked night shift on the ambulance; there were always lights, people, movement. But when she was alone in a closed-in environment like this, the fear crawled up out of her subconscious and scraped on her nerves, built an edgy restlessness.

The storm made it worse, screeching out there like all the pain cries from all the accident victims she'd ever heard combined. So did the fallen tree blocking the lane, trapping them. So did what had happened to Gene Decker. She'd had plenty of experience with death; watched Mom die by degrees, watched strangers die at scenes of mangled metal and flesh or in the ambulance on the way to the hospital. But proximity to cold-blooded murder was something new and unsettling.

She wondered again how Claire was holding up. Not too well, probably, alone in that house with her abusive husband. Maybe she should have gone along with Jay, talked to Claire while he talked to Brian Lomax about the tree. But what could she say to the woman now? Words of comfort from a stranger usually rang hollow; that was a lesson she'd learned early on in her job.

She couldn't sit still. Kept pacing back and forth, waiting for Jay to come back—animal in a cage. Her wineglass was empty; she detoured to the kitchen to refill it. What she really wanted was a martini, or a slug of straight gin without the trimmings, but she'd had two glasses of wine already and if she mixed in hard liquor this early—not even five o'clock yet—she'd be down and out fast. And getting wasted wouldn't accomplish anything anyway, except to give her a hangover to deal with tomorrow. Alcohol was fine for dulling the edges of anxiety, but too much of it did more harm than good.

She'd been in a dull funk ever since she'd made her decision yesterday afternoon and confronted Jay with it. There should've been some sense of relief, of sadness and loss; she ought to be giving some thought to the future, to other decisions she'd be facing. But she seemed mired in that same cold emptiness she'd experienced in the car yesterday. Feeling a kind of bleak disconnection, too; her mind wouldn't stay focused. Why? Because at some level she wasn't convinced a divorce was the right choice after all?

Pace, sip wine, listen to the storm battering the cottage, watch the quivery candlelight and firelight to keep from watching the stationary darkness. She'd never wanted to leave a place more than she wanted out of this one, a feeling as irrational as her borderline nyctophobia. There was really nothing menacing or unpleasant about the cottage or its setting. It was just the wrong place at the wrong time, a symbol, a catalyst. No matter what happened in the future, she knew she would look back on her time here with a sense of loathing.

Rattling at the door, an inrush of wind and wet for a couple of seconds: Jay was back.

He came in breathing hard, jammed the door shut with his body and then threw the bolt. Under the brim of his rain hat, his face was a pale oval slicked with wetness. Shelby went to the kitchen for a dish towel while he shed his rain gear and gloves. The legs of his Levi's were soaked almost to the knee, the rest of his clothing clinging from water that had gotten in under the oilskin.

"What did Lomax say?"

"Didn't talk to him," Jay said as he dried his face and neck. "Couldn't get in past the gates. He had them closed, padlocked with a chain."

"Can't blame him, after what happened to Gene Decker."

"I could've climbed over, but I didn't want to risk it."

"Illegal trespass," she said.

"Yeah. Get my ass shot off." He bent to pick up the sodden hat and coat he'd dropped on the carpet; his breathing was still labored when he straightened.

"Are you all right?"

He answered the question with a dismissive gesture. "Nothing any of us can do in the dark anyway, while it's blowing like this. Have to wait for daylight."

"You'd better get out of those wet clothes and into the shower. There'll be hot water in the tank."

"Okay."

"Here, give me those. I'll hang them up on the porch."

He handed over the coat and hat. "I tried moving the tree with the car before I drove down there," he said. "No use. Too big, and I couldn't get any traction. I don't think Lomax's SUV can move it either. Chain saw's our best bet. He'd better have one."

"We'll worry about that tomorrow. Go on, get into the shower."

"Pour me a glass of wine while I'm in there?"

"Yes."

He went off down the hall, carrying one of the candles. Shelby finished her wine as she poured a glass for Jay. Another glass? Might as well. Three glasses of inexpensive chardonnay should have had her feeling mildly buzzed, but not on this miserable night. The wine might as well have been tap water for all the effect it was having on her.

She relit another couple of snuffed candlewicks, then went to put a pair of logs on the banking fire. It wasn't really cold in there, but she felt chilled just the same. Maybe she'd take a quick shower herself when Jay was finished. Once she'd have just gone in and joined him, to conserve the hot water, but that kind of intimacy was unthinkable now.

The fresh wood began to crackle, radiating heat against her back. But it didn't take the chill away. Bone deep. A mound of blankets and comforters wouldn't make her warm again tonight.

What was taking him so long in there?

Three minutes was his usual shower limit. And he wouldn't use up what was left of the hot water, would he?

She picked up a candle, followed its light into the bedroom.

He was in there, not in the bathroom, dressed in dry trousers and a long-sleeved shirt and sitting slumped on the far side of the bed. The room was cold, very cold—the fire's heat didn't reach back here—but for some reason he'd failed to button the shirt. The candle he'd brought in was on the dresser in front of him; its trembling flame created a restless play of shadows across his face, so that the skin seemed to be rippling like dark water.

"Jay?"

He mumbled something she couldn't hear over the wailing and whining of the storm.

"What's the matter? Aren't you feeling well?"

He winced as if with a sudden spasm, lifted a hand, and then let it drop onto his lap.

Shelby went around the bed, bent to hold the candle up close to his face. It was difficult to tell in the pale light, but his color didn't look good. She pressed the back of her hand against his forehead. Cool, sweaty. And his respiration seemed even more labored.

Red flags. Alarm bells.

"Do you have any pain?"

No answer.

"Dammit, Jay. Do you have any pain?"

"Yes."

"Where?"

He winced again, squeezed his eyes shut.

"Answer me. Where do you hurt?"

". . . Chest. Left arm."

Oh my God!

"Anywhere else?" she asked. "Radiating down your arm, into your back?"

"No."

"Describe the pain to me. Sharp, dull, crushing . . . what?"

"Like a . . . hand squeezing."

"How much trouble getting your breath?"

"A little."

"Nauseous?"

"A little."

"How bad was the pain when it started? Scale of one to ten."

". . . Five, six."

"And now?"

"I don't know . . . not as bad. Three, four."

"Tingling sensation in your fingers?"

"Yes."

"Lie back on the bed, knees up," she said, and helped him into that position. She felt his neck—the veins weren't distended. And there was no pedal edema in his feet and ankles. Quickly she got a blanket from the closet and covered him with it. "Don't move. I'll be right back."

She hurried to the utility porch, swept her raincoat off the hook, found the car keys, and ran outside with the coat draped over her head. Her jump bag was in the Prius's trunk, where she always kept it for work and emergencies. She rushed back inside with it, stopping on the way for another lighted candle. In the bedroom she set the bag on the bureau, opened it.

Stethoscope, blood pressure cuff, pulse oximeter, bottle of chewable baby aspirin. She pulled the blanket down to expose Jay's chest, listened to his lungs with the stethoscope. Slightly wet-sounding. She clipped the oximeter to his index finger, then took his pulse. Rapid, too rapid—125 beats per minute. Rolled up one shirtsleeve, strapped the cuff around his arm, pumped it up, read the pressure gauge by candle flame. 185 over 100. High. Checked the digital reading on the oximeter: 92 percent blood oxygen saturation. Low, on the edge of the danger zone.

"Am I going to die?" he said.

"Not if I can prevent it."

She buttoned his shirt, pulled the blanket back up under his chin.

". . . Pills," he said.

"I'm going to give you aspirin—"

"No . . . in my shaving kit. Prescription vial, little white pills."

Prescription vial, little white pills. "Jesus, Jay—you've been taking nitro-glycerin?"

"Yes."

In the bathroom she rummaged through his kit, found the bottle of nitro tablets. The doctor's name was Prebble—a name she recognized, a well-known South Bay cardiologist. Jay had been to see Prebble, had had heart medication prescribed, and hadn't told her. Why the hell not?

Well, she knew the answer to that, didn't she.

She gave him the baby aspirins first, to make the platelets in the dam-aged artery less sticky, minimize the threat of blood clot formation, and prevent further blockage. When he'd chewed and swallowed them, she shook out two of the tiny nitro tablets and put them under his tongue to dissolve. Then she pawed through her bag again. She had a large portable bottle of oxygen, a Jumbo D, but on a mask it would run at ten to fifteen liters per minute—half an hour at most before it ran dry. Might be better to put him on a cannula instead; it could run at two to six liters per minute, providing a smaller increase over a longer period of time to bring his O_2 level back as close to 100 percent as possible. Depended on what the next blood pressure reading showed.

"How's the pain now?"

"Better. Mostly gone."

"Still having that squeezing sensation?"

"No."

"Difficulty breathing?"

"Not anymore."

"The nausea?"

"Gone."

"All right, good. Just keep still."

Shelby listened to his lungs again; the faint wetness was barely dis-cernible. His pulse rate had slowed and steadied at 80. He wasn't sweating any longer, but his forehead, cheeks, and neck felt even cooler than before. At her touch a shiver went through him. And when she ran fingers over his arm, she felt the goose bumps that had formed there.

She dragged a pillow off the bed, hurried with it into the living room. The fire had begun to bank; she fed it quickly, leaving the fire screen open. She managed to shove the heavy couch over close to the fire, then took three more logs from the wood box and set them on the hearth bricks close by.

Back in the bedroom, she asked Jay if he thought he could sit up.

"I can try."

She helped him into a sitting position. "Any more pain?"

"No."

"Okay. Let's see if you can stand up and walk."

"Where?"

"Out by the fire. You can't stay in here—it's too cold."

She wrapped the blanket around him, holding it closed with one hand. Got him up off the far side of the bed without difficulty; training, all the running and working out she did, had given her the strength to move and support bigger men than Jay. He was a little wobbly, but he didn't sag in her grasp.

"Light-headedness? Discomfort of any kind?"

"No."

She told him to lean on her and take a step, then another. His knees didn't buckle.

"Slow, now," she said, "baby steps."

Out of the bedroom, down the hall, across to the couch. She eased him down on it, arranged the pillow under his head, drew his knees up and tucked the blanket around him. Returned to the bedroom long enough to pull the comforter off the bed, pick up her jump bag and the oximeter and pressure cuff. She covered Jay to the neck with the comforter, leaving one arm exposed, then put the oximeter on his finger and the cuff around his arm and took the readings.

Blood oxygen saturation at 95 percent. Blood pressure at 160 over 80—the nitro tablets had lowered it some but it was still too high. Better go with the cannula. She took it and the Jumbo D and mask from her bag, set the bottle on the floor at the end of the couch farthest from the fire, at the same time running through the litany of questions with him again. The answers he gave were the ones she wanted to hear. She put the cannula on him and started the oxygen flowing.

Stable now—temporarily.

Shelby stood looking down at him, for the first time letting her emotions break through the professional mind-set. A whole conga line of them—cautious relief, compassion, sadness, anger, frustration, tenderness. Love, too, no use denying it. What else would make her eyes start to tear up the way they were now?

You poor damn fool, she thought—and she wasn't sure if she meant Jay or herself or both of them.

SEVENTEEN

MACKLIN HAD KNOWN HE was having a heart attack as soon as the pain started. He'd just gotten out of the shower, dried off, and was putting his shirt on over a dry pair of jeans. It wasn't the hammer blow that would've taken him out right away, just that squeezing sensation and the increased difficulty in getting enough air into his lungs. The bed was as far as he got before the worsening pain and the other symptoms sat him down. He'd tried to call out to Shelby, couldn't seem to raise his voice above a low, feeble cry.

He'd been scared then, still was after all of her ministrations, and yet, strangely, it was a dull, detached kind of fear. He felt disjointed, as if only part of him harbored the anxiety, while the other part was apathetic and resigned. I don't want to die, he thought. But there was a lack of emotion in it, as though the thought had been: I don't want to go out in that storm again.

He lay quiet on the couch, taking in oxygen in slow breaths, watching Shelby watch him. Feeling better now, the symptoms all mostly gone thanks to her. If she hadn't been here when it happened, he'd probably be dead now. He'd never doubted that she was good at her job, but until now he hadn't realized just how calm and skilled she could be under pressure, in a personal crisis. Quite a woman he'd married. A woman he was probably still going to lose, assuming he survived.

"I don't want to leave you alone," Shelby said, "but there's no other choice. You need to be hospitalized ASAP."

"Where'll you go?"

"The Lomaxes. Ask Claire to come stay with you until I can get a medical response unit out here."

"Those locked gates . . . he won't open up for you . . ."

"Let me worry about that. If he has a chain saw, he ought to be able to cut away enough of the tree to let me drive through."

"What if he doesn't have a chain saw?"

Shelby said, "No more talking," and went to quickly don her raincoat, tie the hood under her chin. "While I'm gone I want you to lie still, be as quiet and comfortable as you can. If the oxygen in the cannula runs out before I get back, use the D bottle on the floor there—you know how it works."

He nodded.

"If the fire gets too low and you're feeling well enough, you can get up long enough to toss on another log or two."

Nodded again.

"I'll be back as fast as I can," she said, and in a brief slash of cold air, she was gone.

And he was alone.

He listened to the storm hurl rain on the roof, bludgeon the walls and windows.

The moan of the wind was like a woman in the throes of orgasm. Before long the sense of disjointedness left him and depression moved in in its place, bleak and black. He'd never felt more helpless. Or less of a man. Swaddled up like a baby waiting to be coddled, burped, and diaper-changed.

He almost wished the coronary had killed him—a sudden crushing blow, then straight out of his misery. But no, that would've been too easy, too quick. This way he was facing a future filled with hospitals, doctors' offices, reduced activities, bland food, loneliness if Shelby went through with the divorce and a life of dependency whether she did or didn't, and no worthwhile job prospect in either case because who'd hire a man with one foot in the grave? Months, years of suffering, causing suffering, until another attack took him out or he took himself out. Hell, why not just get up and run around in circles naked until his heart quit beating from the strain, put an end to it right here and now?

Stupid thought. Selfish. He was a long way from the suicide stage yet; self-preservation was still too strong in him. More important, he couldn't do a thing like that to Shelby. Not now, after all she'd done and was out there doing to try to save his sorry ass.

Bitterly he found himself thinking back to the week before Christmas. He'd had the arrhythmia and shortness of breath for a while before they finally alarmed him enough to do what Shelby's urgings hadn't—send him to his doctor, who had shuttled him on to the cardiologist, Dr. Prebble. A stress test confirmed the diminished capacity in his heart. So then they'd put him in the hospital overnight—he'd called Shelby and lied to her about an all-night poker game at Ben Coulter's—and administered a bunch of tests, including an echocardiogram to determine the location of the blockage. There'd been some talk about "cathing" him—inserting a minicam in his veins and running it up into the heart to look for other blockages—but the cardiologist had finally determined that the procedure wasn't necessary.

Diagnosis: CAD—coronary artery disease. How could a thirty-five-year-old man have CAD? That had been his first reaction. Age was no factor in heart disease, Prebble had told him; people of any age could have it. Usually it was genetic, but not always. His reaction to that had been the typically self-pitying one: Why me? Took a while to get over it and reconcile himself, but he'd managed it. Or thought he had until now.

His CAD required bypass surgery, double, triple, maybe quadruple, they couldn't be sure until they opened him up and inspected the damage. Prebble's dry, professional voice telling him this, and then explaining what the surgery entailed: ten-inch-long incision in the middle of his chest, his breastbone separated to create an opening to view the heart and aorta; connection to a heart-lung bypass machine that circulated the blood through his body during surgery; the possible use of the saphenous vein in his leg, or an internal mammary artery, or the radial artery in his wrist

to create grafts around the blocked areas; then his breastbone recon-
nected with wire and the incision sewn up. Five to seven days in the
hospital, the first few hours in ICU, and the balance of his recovery at
home. Good as new in time . . . maybe. If he didn't die on the operating
table from traveling blood clots or immediately afterward from infection
or some other post-op risk. Or end up having a fatal myocardial infarc-
tion despite the bypass.

Merry Christmas, Mr. Macklin. Happy New Year.

Dr. Prebble had wanted him to have the operation right away. He'd
balked. Couldn't it wait until after the holidays? Yes, though it was always best to act quickly in cases like his. Talk it over with your wife, the
doctor told him, before you decide definitely to wait. He said he would,
but he couldn't, couldn't, couldn't. Instead he'd lied to Prebble, saying he
and Shelby both agreed he should wait until after the first of the year. That
way, he figured he could enjoy what might be his last Christmas and his
last auld lang syne, accept Ben's offer to use the cottage in between . . .
stick his head in the sand like an ostrich. The risk in waiting was relatively small as long as he didn't overexert himself, watched his diet and
cut down on his alcohol consumption, got plenty of rest, and faithfully
took the little white nitroglycerine tablets Dr. Prebble prescribed. That
was what Prebble had told him and what he'd made himself believe.

And they'd both been wrong.

And now he and Shelby were paying the price.

EIGHTEEN

IT WAS FULL DARK now, the night alive with shifting, rain-drenched shadows just outside the reach of the Prius's headlights. The twin rays seemed to reflect off rather than penetrate the downpour, tingeing the wild scurry of clouds with a faint luminescence. The surface of the lane between the cottage and the Lomax house was heavily puddled and greasy; in Shelby's haste she nearly lost control on the one slight curve, turned into the skid just in time. Thank God there were no more toppled trees or other obstacles in her path.

She pulled up at an angle in front of the closed gates, so that the headlight shine illuminated them. Left the engine running and the lights on. Thunder made a drumroll riff in the distance; a few seconds later a lightning fork etched jagged yellow patterns on the canopy of darkness above the ocean. The lightning burst lit up the house for an instant, too, gave it a surreal look like something out of a neo-Gothic horror film.

She took hold of the gates, shoved them apart as far as they would go so she could see through to the front of the house. Dark. The flickers of light she'd seen as she drove up were at the rear. The Lomaxes must be in the sunken living room with logs blazing in that massive stone fireplace; ragged streamers of smoke poured from the chimney, faintly visible before the gale tore them apart.

At first she thought there was enough separation between the two gate halves for her to slide her body through, but as soon as she tried it she knew she'd only succeed in getting herself stuck. Up and over, then—no time to waste. The gates were only six feet high and she'd always been adept at climbing.

She got one foot on the chain, both hands on the soaked top bar of one half; pulled herself up, swung her legs over, managed to scramble down inside without hurting herself. The flashlight was in the slash pocket of her raincoat; she dragged it out, switched it on.

The deluge was so intense it was like trying to push her way through something semisolid. A wind surge sent a three-foot-long branch skittering against her legs as she followed the beam across the parking area, nearly tripping her. She braced herself and kicked it away; plowed ahead to the porch.

More than a minute of leaning on the doorbell brought no response. She tried hammering on the door with her fist, thumbing the bell again at the same time. Futile. The storm made too much noise for her to hear anything from inside, but she had the prickly feeling of being watched through the peephole. She lifted her face close to the convex glass eye, mouthed the words, "Help, I need help."

Nothing. The door stayed shut.

Damn Brian Lomax and his paranoia!

Desperation drove her off the porch, around onto a brick path that paralleled the south side of the house. Thick manzanita shrubs made close borders along the path, their thin, coarse branches scraping at her as she passed. Three windows on that side, all of them shaded, only the farthest one shielding light. She pawed through the shrubbery and tried the latches on all three, knowing they'd be locked tight, doing it anyway.

When she reached the back corner, the flash beam showed her a low, railed deck running the width of the house, steps bisecting it in the center. As she stepped out and around the end of the deck, a sharp burst of bitter-cold wind and rain shoved her off-balance against the planking; she had to hang on to the railing posts to remain upright.

She aimed the torch at the back wall. The drapes were drawn across picture windows and sliding glass door, but behind the door there was a thin gap where the cloth folds didn't quite meet, letting a strip of light leak out.

Up the steps, her body bent almost double; the squall, like a hand in her back, thrust her forward against the door glass. She darkened the flash and slipped it into her pocket; sleeved her eyes clear and sluiced water off the glass so she could squint through the gap between the drapes.

Brian Lomax was standing statuelike near the fireplace, his big hands flat against his sides—directly in her line of sight. Tucked into the waistband of his trousers was the handgun he'd displayed two nights ago. If Claire was anywhere in the room, Shelby couldn't see her.

She clung to the door handle with one gloved hand, made a fist of the other and banged it hard on the glass, making the pane rattle in its metal frame. No response. She ground her molars in frustration, peered through the opening again. Lomax still stood in the same spot, in the same posture, his beard-shadowed face like a stone mask.

She had a quick flash of Jay lying sick and alone in the dwindling firelight, and a frenzied wildness took hold of her. She pounded on the glass with all her strength, she didn't care if she shattered or spiderwebbed it. Kept pounding, pounding. How long could he resist opening the door?

Not much longer. All at once the drapes were swept back and Lomax was there, staring out at her through the glass.

But he still didn't open the door.

Again she mouthed the words, "Help, I need help," and added a "please" that had the taste of camphor on her tongue.

Lomax kept on staring, shaking his head now.

Furious, Shelby hammered on the glass again, directly in front of that stone-mask face. She kept it up until the mask began to slip a little—mouth and jaw tightening, eyelids pinching down. Finally got through to him, made him realize that ignoring her wouldn't make her go away. He reached down to snap the lock free, slid the door open a few inches. Blocking it with his body, the fingers of his right hand resting on the automatic's handle: He wasn't going to let her into the house.

"What's the idea? I could have you arrested for trespassing."

She could barely hear him over the storm's shrieks and wails. Rain blew in past her, splattering droplets against his face; he didn't seem to notice. She leaned up into the opening, close enough to smell the alcohol on his breath. His eyes had a hard fixity, like cat's-eye marbles, but he didn't seem to be drunk—at least not drunk enough to slur his words or impair his ability to function.

"Let me come in."

"No. What do you want?"

"I need your help, yours and Claire's."

". . . What kind of help?"

"My husband's had a heart attack." Shouting to make sure he heard and understood what she was saying. "I've got him stabilized for now, but I can't go for help because the lane's blocked on the far side of the cottage—the storm blew a tree down across it."

Nothing changed in Lomax's expression. His voice remained flat and cold when he said, "That's too bad. What do you want me to do?"

"You have a chain saw? I thought maybe you could—"

"No. No chain saw."

He was lying. She couldn't have said how she knew, but she was immediately sure of it—lying through his teeth. Why, for God's sake?

"All right, then, we can try moving the tree with your SUV—"

"No."

"What do you mean, no?"

"It's not any good for that kind of thing. Sits too high."

"You haven't even seen the fucking tree! Come with me, take a look."

"No. There's no use in it."

Shelby controlled a savage impulse to reach through, grab him by the throat and choke him. "Listen to me," she shouted. "Jay could die if he doesn't get emergency treatment ASAP. You understand? He could die!"

"I'm sorry, there's nothing I can do."

"Yes there is." Spitting the words at him now. "You or Claire can stay with him until I get back with a doctor or EMS unit. Keep the fire going so he stays warm— Why the hell are you shaking your head?"

"Claire's sick. I can't let her go out in this storm."

"Sick?"

"She's in bed. Flu or something."

"Then you come stay with Jay."

"I can't do that. I can't leave her alone."

"God damn you, can't you get it through your head my husband might die unless—"

Lomax said, "There's nothing we can do. Get off my property," and backed up a step and slid the door shut and snapped the drapes closed again, tight this time—all in one continuous motion.

A surge of impotent rage made her yell, "You miserable son of a bitch!" and beat on the glass a few more times. Then her control came back, and along with it a redoubled need for urgency.

She shoved away from the glass, thumbed the flashlight back on, fought the wind down the steps and back around to the brick path. A bone-white dazzle of lightning flashed as she emerged onto the parking area, followed by more rolling echoes of thunder when she reached the gates. Up and over and back into the car. Moving again.

The rage still stalked her mind. What kind of man was Brian Lomax, to blow her off the way he had? Sub-fucking-human. If Jay died or suffered permanent damage because of him, she'd make him pay somehow. There wasn't anything the law could do to him—he was within his rights to refuse her admission to his house, refuse to help her because his wife was "sick"; could even bring charges against her for illegal trespass. But she could let the world know how he'd acted tonight. Make *him* suffer through the media if not in a courtroom.

She drove too fast back to the cottage, ran stumbling through the open gate and slipped quickly inside. Candle flames guttered; she half noticed that some of the candles were already melting into puddles of red and green wax. The focus of her attention was Jay. He was lying as she'd left him with the blanket and comforter pulled up beneath his chin, the cannula still clipped into his nose. Conscious and alert: He raised his head as she hurried across the room.

He asked in a scratchy voice, "What happened?"

Shelby told him in clipped sentences. "I think Lomax was lying. About the chain saw, about Claire being sick."

"Bastard beat her up again."

"Probably." She went to one knee beside the couch. "How do you feel?"

"Better."

"Pain anywhere? Discomfort?"

"No."

His voice sounded strong, his color was good and his eyes clear. She removed her gloves, laid a hand on his forehead. Dry and warm, but not feverish. She checked his vital signs again. Lungs clear. Blood oxygen saturation up to 98 percent. Blood pressure holding now at 125 over 78.

The fire was already burning low. She stoked it with the last three small logs in the wood box, leaving the ones on the hearth where they lay. When she turned back to Jay, he said, "There's something I have to tell you."

"It can wait. Are you thirsty?"

"A little, but—"

She went to the kitchen, filled a small tumbler, and brought it back. Raised his head, let him swallow a little, then set the glass on the floor within his reach.

"You need to use the bathroom?"

"No."

"Good." She indicated the glass. "Small sips when you want more, so you won't need to pee."

"Shel, listen," he said, his voice earnest now. In the firelight the planes of his face had a bronze cast and his eyes were like black opals. "This isn't the first time I've had chest pains. I've been seeing a cardiologist."

"Dr. Prebble. The nitroglycerine tablets. How long?"

"The week before Christmas. He ran tests . . . told me I need to have bypass surgery. He wanted to do it right away, but I said no, wait until after the first of the year. I didn't want to spoil the holidays for us."

Spoil the holidays. Good God.

She said, keeping her voice even, "Is that the real reason for this trip?"

"Yes. It seemed like a good idea . . . time alone together, maybe the last good time we'd ever have. Wasn't that I thought I'd die, it was the way things will be after the surgery. Bad heart, unable to work, financial drain. I've been a burden on you so long, it can only get worse . . ."

"Were you trying to drive me away?"

"No. I knew you'd stay with me, at least for a while."

"Out of pity? Is that the kind of person you think I am?"

"God, no. It's just that . . . I can't stand the thought of you having to take care of me the rest of my life. I may not be much of a man anymore, but I've got some pride left."

Pride? Stupid male ego.

"Why couldn't you tell me all this before?"

"I wanted to. I tried to. I've never meant to keep anything from you, but I didn't have the words . . . no, that's not true, I had the words but I couldn't say them. Some kind of mental block . . . I don't know, I can't explain it . . ."

He was getting himself worked up, the worst possible thing for his heart. "All right, that's enough," she said. "There's no time for any more of this now. I have to go and you have to rest."

". . . What're you going to do?"

"The only thing I can do." She had her raincoat rebuttoned, was pulling the hood up over her head again. "Hoof it out to the highway and flag down the first car that comes along. Or walk all the way into Seacrest if I have to."

"Dangerous," he said. "Woman alone on a night like this, lunatic running around loose—"

"I can take care of myself." Can of Mace in her purse, self-defense tactics learned and internalized in a police-sponsored class she'd taken a few years ago. And the flashlight to keep the darkness from swallowing her.

He said, "I love you, Shel. No matter what happens, I'll always love you."

She said, "I love you, too," because it was what he wanted to hear and it would help keep him calm, let him rest more easily. Then she turned quickly away, went back out into the hell-black night.

NINETEEN

MACKLIN DOZED. PULSES OF heat from the stoked-up fire, the smother of the blanket and comforter, the immobility, the recuperative demands of his body, the now-monotonous ravings of the storm—all combined to push him toward the edge of a deeper sleep. He struggled against it, blinking himself awake every time he reached the edge, because sleep was also an easy escape, another way of hiding, and he wasn't going to hide anymore.

How much time had passed since Shelby left the second time? It seemed like an hour, probably wasn't more than a handful of minutes. Out there braving the storm and her fear of the dark and Christ knew what else for him, while he lay here warm and comfortable and waited for her to come back with help.

The black despair had left him a while ago, replaced by a resignation that was no longer quite so fatalistic. Whatever happened, it was pretty much out of his hands now.

One good thing about the heart attack: He'd finally been able to tell Shelby about Dr. Prebble and the need for the bypass operation. The words, so clogged and clotted in him every time he'd tried before, had come spewing out tonight like dammed-up water released through a spillway. And he had a sense that the spillway would remain open; that the attack had rewired him somehow and if he was given the chance, he'd be able to confide some of the other private thoughts and feelings that he'd kept locked away from her. Even though it had taken a freakish set of circumstances and a faceup look at his own mortality to make it happen, it let him feel a little better about himself, gave him a measure of hope.

His eyelids grew heavy, too heavy to keep raised. He dozed again. Snapped awake. Dozed.

Slept, in spite of himself.

And rode the nightmare again.

The same, yet not the same this time. All the familiar components, only they were broken up into out-of-sequence fragments, like film clips spliced together by a child or a drunk. It wasn't as though he were living it but as if he were an observer watching the spliced bits unroll across a screen. The terror was there, but muted and without the usual ravaging intensity. And it didn't end with those yellow fangs devouring his body while his torn-off head looked on in horror; it ended with the monster's roaring words jumbled but recognizable, sentence chunks that no longer fell like whispers but like cushioned blows against his ears.

For the first time he didn't scream himself free of it; he was simply awake, tense, but not sweating or shaking or struggling for breath. An accelerated pulsebeat was the only physical effect. The dream creature's words echoed and reechoed in his mind. He lay piecing them together, arranging them in a semblance of order, until with a mixture of awe and anger he began to comprehend what they meant, what the nightmare signified and why he'd kept having it all these years—

The sound of the door opening, the sudden inrush of frigid air, chased it all aside, compartmentalized it.

Shelby, he thought. Back already.

He lifted his head, and then blinked and stared because it wasn't Shelby who came stalking across the room, dripping rainwater and leaving muddy splotches on the carpet, waving a lighted torch as if it were a weapon.

Brian Lomax.

There was no expression on the man's blocky, beard-stubbled face, but his eyes had a distended look, as if from some internal pressure. Crazy eyes.

Crazy drunk, Macklin thought. They held briefly on him, then shifted and darted from one point to another, following the erratic, tracerlike patterns of the flash beam around the living room, over into the kitchen. Lomax wore a heavy mackinaw buttoned to the throat but no hat; rain glistened on his spiky hair and pink scalp, dribbled down around the edges of his mouth and off the tip of his chin.

"Where's my wife?" he said.

It wasn't what Macklin expected to hear. He pushed himself up gingerly until he was half sitting against the pillows. "How should I know?"

"Has she been here?"

"No. I thought she was sick, couldn't leave the house—"

"That's right, she is, but she got out anyway. The front door . . . damn her, she must've found an extra key."

That sounded as if Lomax had been holding her against her will. Beating on her again, probably, keeping her prisoner—and now she'd managed to escape. If he found her, then what?

Macklin said, trying to keep his voice neutral, "What makes you think she'd come here?"

"No place else for her to go."

Except out to the highway. But if that thought hadn't occurred to Lomax, Macklin wasn't about to put it into his head.

He said, "Then she must be hiding somewhere in the woods."

"We'll see about that."

Lomax took the flashlight into the kitchen, then down the hall. The drumbeat of rain on the roof seemed to have let up a little; the gusts buffeting the cottage weren't quite as strong as before. Macklin could hear him in the guest bedroom, then the master bedroom, banging closet doors. Probably down on all fours, too, looking under the beds.

He sat up a little straighter, swung one leg off the couch. But he was afraid to try getting up. And what could he do if he did, against a healthy man of Lomax's bulk? For all he knew, the bastard had brought that gun of his with him.

When Lomax came stalking back into the room, Macklin said,

"What's the idea, barging in here like this? My wife told you I had a heart attack—"

"Might be dying, she said. You look all right to me."

"You're not an EMT."

"She's the reason Claire got out."

". . . What're you talking about?"

"Your damn wife. Trespassing on my property, pounding on the doors and windows, distracting me. It's her fault."

Nothing would ever be Lomax's fault, always somebody else's. "Yeah, well, you're the one trespassing now."

"No. She wanted me to come here."

"Not like this, she didn't."

"Where is she?"

"Where do you think, Lomax? Gone to bring help because you refused to do anything—"

"Take Claire with her?"

"What?"

"Your wife. She took Claire with her when she left, didn't she?"

"No. Why would she do that? She wanted Claire to stay with me—"

"Don't lie to me. Has my wife been here or not?"

"I just told you she hasn't."

"And I told *you* I have to find her."

"Why? So you can beat on her some more?"

Jerkily, Lomax moved a few steps closer to the couch. The pupils of his eyes gleamed like fragments of jet in the half light; fireglow struck spark-like glints from them. "So neither of you has seen her," he said.

"Not since Shelby ran into her on the beach."

"The beach? When? When was that?"

"Day before yesterday."

"What time?"

"What difference does that make?"

"What time!"

"Late morning, after your sister left."

"Late morning . . . yes, sure, all right. What'd Claire tell her?"

"She didn't have to tell her anything. Shelby has eyes—one look at what you did to her face was enough."

"Claire had it coming. If it wasn't for her . . ." Lomax bared his teeth like a feral dog, smacked the flashlight hard into the palm of his other hand. The knobs of muscle along the sides of his jaw were the size of walnuts. Crazy, all right. Those bulging eyes . . . some sort of psychotic break? "I've got to find her before it's too late."

"Too late for what?"

"If she shows up here, you tell her she better go home and stay there if she knows what's good for her. You understand?"

No use arguing with him. You couldn't reason with a man like Lomax when he was half drunk and worked up like this. Be a mistake to go on trying.

"Yeah, I understand."

Lomax spun on his heel, stalked across the room, vanished as quickly as he'd appeared.

But he didn't pull the door tight shut behind him. The wind hurled it open, set it banging against the closet door behind it. Candle flames guttered, blew out in the swirls of moist air.

Son of a bitch!

Macklin had no choice; he *had* to get up, walk over there, shut that door before the cold ate up all the room's heat.

He threw the comforter down and swung both legs off the couch, planted his slippered feet flat on the floor. Slow, deep breath. Both hands on the couch arm, turn his body, shove up . . . slow . . . that's it, up, all the way up . . . and standing, half turned, leaning on his hands.

A little weak in the knees, but not too bad. Another deep breath. No pain or dizziness, his breathing under control. Okay. Weight off his hands and arms . . . straighten, slow. Experimental step to make sure of his balance, holding the blanket tight around him with both hands. Okay.

Walk.

Left foot, right foot, fighting the urge to hurry. Straight ahead into the wet and cold, teeth gritted, the blanket and the tails of his robe flapping against his legs. Half expecting the squeezing to start again, but it didn't happen. Still breathing without difficulty. And surprisingly steady on his pins, despite the still-sharp prod of the wind, the icy drops blowing into his face.

Three more steps, two, one . . . there. He caught hold of the door, tried to throw it shut; the wind threw it back at him. Come on, Macklin. Get a grip on the knob, lean your shoulder against the door and shove it closed. Even with a bad heart you're stronger than the goddamn wind—

He was turning his body, starting to push on the door, when the face appeared out of the roiling darkness outside.

Witch's face: slick-sheened and pasty white, one cheekbone bruised, lips split and cracked, tangled strands of hair stuck down or streaming in all directions, eyes like black holes. Startling him—his heart thumped and skipped a beat, his breath caught in the back of his throat.

A dripping hand clawed a hold on the edge of the door, the face loomed closer. Not a witch's face—the face of terror. And a voice to match: "Let me in . . . please, *please*, before he comes back."

First Lomax and now his wife.

TWENTY

SHELBY DROVE DOWN TO where the fallen tree blocked the lane, even though the distance was only fifty yards or so. The need for urgency was a constant prod. Jay's condition didn't seem to be as bad as she'd feared initially, but there was no way to tell for sure without a battery of hospital tests. All too often heart attacks came in pairs or bunches, spaced minutes as well as hours apart. He could have another at any time, go into cardiac arrest. And even if that didn't happen tonight, the damage that had already been done might be severe enough to be life-threatening at some point in the future.

Mad as hell at him for withholding Dr. Prebble's diagnosis from her. Didn't want to spoil the holidays for either of them. Jesus! If he'd only told her as soon as he found out, none of this coastal horror show would have happened. Right now her love for him was tempered with a thinly diluted hostility. *I've been a burden on you so long, it can only get worse . . .* Yes, it probably would get worse before it got better, if it ever could.

Shelby Hunter Macklin: wife, caregiver, angel of mercy, her husband's keeper.

The fallen tree was bigger than she'd expected, thick-boled, its jutting limbs and branches like fragmented bones in the rain. She eased the Prius to a stop close to the vine-choked trunk. Switched on the flash before she shut off the engine and headlights and got out into the squall.

She tracked the beam to the upper end of the tree. There was a spot near the collapsed section of the estate fence where she thought she could climb over, but too many snags and splintered edges forced her back. Damn! She took the light down to the snapped-off end, found a way to get around it there by plowing through some sodden undergrowth.

On the far side, the pavement and what bordered it on both sides were indistinguishable beyond the light's reach. Shelby aimed her gaze and the shaft downward a few feet in front of her, focusing on the moving circle of radiance as she followed it along the lane.

When she'd gone a hundred yards or so, around a jog in the lane, a tracery of lightning showed her a dark shape on the side of the road ahead. She lifted the flash, hurrying now, not quite believing her eyes until the beam reached far enough to reflect off streaming metal and glass surfaces.

Car.

Better than that, a county sheriff's cruiser.

Finally, a piece of good luck!

She half ran to the cruiser. Its flasher bar was unlighted, the interior also dark. At the driver's window she laid the lens close to the glass, cleared it with her palm and squinted to peer inside. The front seat was empty, the barrel of a Remington shotgun jutting up like a phallus from its vertical mount. She moved back to shine the light through the rear window. The area behind the separating mesh partition was as empty as the front.

Where was the deputy?

Why would he leave his cruiser parked here like this?

She swung the torch around in a slow circle. Vague shapes jumped out, vanished again. Rain-heavy tree branches bobbing and weaving in the wind. The verge-flooded lane. The estate fence and closed entrance gates. All of it storm-tossed, barren, like pieces of nowhere.

Maybe there was something wrong with the cruiser and the deputy had pulled it in here and then gone on foot to the highway— No, that couldn't be it. The highway was several hundred yards from here. He wouldn't have driven in this far; he'd have radioed for help and waited out there in the cruiser, dry.

Radio, she thought.

She pivoted back to the driver's door and tried the handle, expecting to find it locked. It wasn't. She let out a stuttery breath and stopped thinking about the missing deputy; pulled the door open and slid quickly inside, closing it after her.

The dome light showed her the position of the radio and its microphone. She'd used communications of this kind for ten years, the codes up here wouldn't be much different from those she was used to; all she had to do was contact the dispatcher and report the abandoned cruiser, request immediate assistance and a medical response unit. She set her purse down on the passenger seat, caught up the microphone, flipped a toggle—

The driver's door was suddenly yanked open from outside.

A hand reached in and snatched the microphone from her, a wind-bent voice said, "No, you don't," and before she could turn her head all the way around, a pair of powerful arms had encircled her body and were dragging her backward out of the cruiser.

TWENTY-ONE

MACKLIN LET CLAIRE LOMAX inside, shouldered the door shut behind her. And this time reached down to throw the bolt lock.

"Oh God, thank you."

She stood trembling with her arms crossed over her breasts. She was wet through to the skin; the clothing she wore—a down jacket over some kind of shirt, a pair of Levi's, and sneakers—were all drenched and streaming. The injuries to her face were worse than Shelby had described, probably the result of a second or even a third beating over the past two days. Her terror was as naked as any Macklin had ever witnessed.

"How long were you out there?"

"I climbed up just before Brian got here." The words had a staccato sound because of the way her teeth were chattering. "If I hadn't seen him before he saw me . . . I hid behind one of the sheds until I saw him leave."

"Climbed up? You don't mean from the beach?"

"Yes, the beach."

"In this storm, with those big waves down there?"

"There wasn't any other way. He had the front gates locked . . . I was afraid he'd catch me if I tried to get out there."

"You could've been battered against the rocks, washed out to sea."

"I almost was. A wave knocked me down, I lost the flashlight I had . . ."

A tremor shook her, strong enough to create a rippling effect like an aftershock. "Never mind that now. We have to get away from here before he comes back."

Macklin moved over to lean against the breakfast bar. He still felt pretty good, almost normal in fact, as if he hadn't had a cardiac episode. Illusion. He'd had one, all right.

"We can't do that," he said.

"Why can't we? You don't understand, he'll kill me if he finds me. He *will*, I'm not making that up—" She broke off, her gaze taking in the shadowy emptiness of the room. Most of the candles were out now, all except one on the counter beneath the bar top and another in the kitchen; the light from the waning fire tinged the murkiness with an eerie glow. "Where's your wife?"

"Gone for help."

"Help? In your car? Your car's not here?"

"Outside somewhere, but the storm blew a tree down across the lane. There's no way past it except on foot."

She stared at him, disbelieving. "You mean we're trapped?"

"Until Shelby gets back, yes."

"No, no, no!" Claire's head shook loosely from side to side like a bobble doll's—an involuntary reflex that went on for several seconds. Then she made a little keening sound and said in desperate tones, "Have you got a gun?"

"No."

"Not even a rifle?"

"Nothing like that."

"Shit! He'll shoot me if he comes back, don't you understand that? He'll shoot both of us!"

"He didn't seem that crazy," Macklin lied.

"But he is. You don't know how crazy."

She stumbled around the breakfast bar into the kitchen, began rummaging through drawers. He knew what she was after, saw two of them in her hand when she came back into the living room—butcher knives.

"Those won't do any good against that automatic of his."

"We have to have *something* . . ." She extended one of the knives, and when he didn't take it she dropped it clattering onto the bar. She seemed to be seeing him clearly then for the first time, the blanket he held tight-wrapped around him; a frown put lines and ridges in her ravaged face. "You said Shelby went for help. Why? What happened?"

"I had a cardiac episode."

"You . . . what?"

"Heart attack. Mild one, I hope, but—"

Laughter burst out of her, sudden and hysterical. Witch's sounds to go with the witch's face, like mad echoes of the storm outside. It lasted ten seconds or so, morphed abruptly into sobs that shook her whole body. She moved away from him, sank into one of the dinette chairs. Sat slumped there with the butcher knife in her lap, shaking and sobbing.

There was nothing he could do, no comfort he could give her. He said, "You'd better get out of those wet clothes. Shelby's about your size—put on something of hers."

Claire didn't seem to hear him. Lost in the clutches of her fear.

He had to say it twice more before the words penetrated. "Go on. Take a candle into the bedroom, the one on the right. Her clothes are in the closet."

Another tremor prodded her off the chair. He handed her the candle from the bar; she peered at it, peered at him. Illuminated by its flame, the whites of her eyes had the look of clabbered milk spiderwebbed with thin red veins.

When she'd gone to the bedroom, Macklin walked slowly across to the hearth. Among the set of black-iron fire tools was a heavy poker with a hooked protrusion at the end; he caught it up, hefted it. Not much of a weapon against a handgun, but better than a knife would be. He leaned forward gingerly to poke the fire, then brought the poker back to the bar and rested a hip on one of the stools. Still feeling okay. The last of the weakness in his legs had disappeared.

Claire seemed to have marshaled her defenses when she came back wearing one of Shelby's sweaters and a pair of her jeans, the towel-dried blonde hair frizzed around her head like a fright wig. The terror in her eyes wasn't quite as stark now.

She said in a scooped-out voice, "You don't look like you've had a heart attack."

"Maybe not, but that's what happened."

"But you're only . . . what, forty?"

"Thirty-five. But age doesn't have much to do with it," Macklin said. "I have a blocked artery . . . need surgery after the holidays. Too much stress brought it on."

Claire moved over by the fire. He told her to add another log from the dwindling supply in the woodpile; she did that, then stood off to one side, slumped and sag-shouldered with her arms hugging her breasts. Like a woman hanging from a nail.

"Everything happens at once," she said. "Brian, the storm, lane blocked, medical emergency . . . it's like a nightmare."

Yeah, Macklin thought, only this is the real thing.

"I don't want to die," she said.

"You're not going to die, not tonight."

"He's coming back."

"I don't think so."

"He is. You don't know him."

"There're dozens of places you could've gone, could've hidden. He can't look everywhere in the dark. He won't know you're here."

"He'll know. He'll be back."

"If he does, we'll be ready for him."

"Stab him? Beat his head in with that poker?"

"If we can catch him by surprise."

"I'm hurt, you're sick, we won't stand a chance. He'll kill us."

Macklin said, "No, he won't," making it sound definite. Then, "Why are you so sure he wants you dead?"

"He swore he'd do it if I told on him, tried to leave him. But I knew he was planning to do it anyway, no matter what I said or did. Tonight, tomorrow . . . that's why he was keeping me prisoner. Working himself up to it. I could see it in his eyes. It's the only way he can ever be sure."

"Sure of what?"

She didn't answer. He couldn't be certain in the weak light but he thought her eyes were shut.

He stood, slowly walked to the couch. Leaned against it and asked again, "The only way he can ever be sure of what, Claire?"

"That he'll be safe."

"From what?"

"The police." Whispering now.

"Why would the police want him?"

"For murder."

". . . Murder? Whose murder?"

"Gene," she said. "He's the one who killed Gene."

TWENTY-TWO

T HE SUDDENNESS OF THE attack was alarming. Shelby's first thought was that it must be the sheriff's deputy, that he was protecting county property and would release her once he had her clear of the cruiser, but it didn't happen that way. He twisted her sideways, kicked the door shut to cut off the dome light, and kept right on dragging her backward across the blacktop.

Storm-blurred voice in her ear: "Don't fight me."

The words had the opposite effect on her: They brought a rush of fear, and with it the instinctive responses taught by her self-defense training. She writhed in the strong grip, kicking backward and flailing with the flashlight.

One of the hands let go of her long enough to punch up on her wrist; the force of the blow ripped the torch loose, sent it up and away in a spinning arc that threw the cruiser into weird relief for an instant before it smashed into the roadbed and went out. Thick, unrelieved blackness closed in around her and the man who held her pinned against him.

Her fear ratcheted up a notch. She fought frantically, couldn't break free. The blurred voice came again, harsh now, the same words, "Don't fight me!" His breath was hot in her ear, the hard-muscled contours of his body straining against hers, the powerful hands still pulling her backward but also trying to turn her toward him. It was as if she were in a mad lover's embrace, being drawn deeper into the roiling black, into a void, an abyss.

Shelby kicked backward again, missed his wide-spread legs the first time, connected the second. The heel-blow on his shin hurt him enough to make him relax his grip. Squirming, she drove an elbow into some soft part of him that brought a grunt and finally allowed her to tear free.

She ran.

He shouted something behind her, a command or threat that was lost in the gibbering wind.

Ran in a blind zigzag, sawing the air in front of her with both hands.

The slick, pine-needled surface of the lane was under her feet and then it wasn't. Flowing stream of water, ankle deep, that slowed her down to a high-stepping slog. The shadow shape of a tree loomed in front of her; she dodged just in time to avoid running into it head on, a move that brought her out of the water and onto solid ground again. When she caught hold of the bole to thrust herself around it, the rough bark ripped a slit in her glove and scraped skin off her palm.

Behind her an arrow of light sliced the darkness. But it didn't come anywhere near her and she almost welcomed it, for it drove away some of the claustrophobic panic and showed her where she was—at the edge of the woods on the inland side of the lane.

The pines grew close together here, the spaces between them crowded with ground cover, deadfalls. She plowed through the undergrowth, managed to sidestep another tree. Something unseen clutched at her foot like bony fingers, toppled her to one knee a second or two before the flash beam swept past overhead, close this time. He hadn't seen her because the light kept seesawing back and forth, but he'd guessed her approximate location.

Shelby clawed at the nearest tree, regained her feet and stumbled ahead, the heavy resinous smell of the pines clogging her nostrils, her breath coming in ragged little gasps. Cold, wet, confused. Angry, too—furious.

Why would a deputy sheriff attack her, chase her? Why would *anybody* do something like this?

The wind was an ally now: He couldn't hear the sounds she made over its whistles and whines. And he still couldn't find her with the light. She kept moving, trying to stay close to the lane. Escape would be easier if she veered deeper into the woods; she could hide somewhere, under bushes, one of the deadfalls . . . he'd never find her, give up searching eventually and go away—

No. It'd be even easier to get lost in there. She could wander around for hours, the whole night, looking for a way out of the blackness with the nyctophobia-induced panic slowly suffocating her.

Her objective had to be the same as before: get away somehow and make it out to the highway. There'd be places to hide until a car came along that she could flag down. Help for her, help for Jay—

One sliding foot caught in a tangle of undergrowth, threw her down again . . . into a nest of ferns this time, the fronds brushing cold and wet across her face. Her right hand slid into something yielding that had a clammy, spongy feel against her scraped palm and made her recoil. Dead animal? But then she realized it had crumbled apart at her touch and knew what it was—one of a cluster of fat mushrooms or toadstools growing in the soggy earth under the ferns.

When she looked up, the light was bright and moving at right angles to where she lay. He was only a few yards away, walking along the flooded edge of the blacktop, probing for her in the timber.

Shelby crawled forward, deeper among the ferns, and then lay motionless. The rain-fuzzed light was ahead of her now, moving away, until all she could see of it were quick little flicks among the trees . . .

After a few seconds it brightened again: He'd turned and was coming back. But he didn't find her this time, either. The beam slid on past, diminishing as he moved.

And then suddenly it was gone, switched off.

Utter blackness brought another surge of fear, like an electric shock on raw nerve endings. She had the same feeling of breathlessness Jay must have experienced earlier; it took an effort of will to keep from hyperventilating.

I won't give into this, I won't!

She shoved onto her knees, crawled until her hand touched the wet base of a tree. The trunk was thickly twined with some kind of vine . . . ivy, poison oak. She grasped handfuls of it, pulled herself upright and leaned against the wet leaves. The crying wind, rainwater plopping all around her—that was all she could hear except for the blood-beat in her ears.

Why had he shut off the flashlight?

Where was he, what was he doing in the dark?

Minutes passed . . . what seemed like minutes. She crouched against the tree, wet to the skin and shivering, her toes numb inside her sodden running shoes. Fighting to keep the phobic terror from overwhelming her. The lane . . . where was the lane? It had to be close on her right. But if she went out there into the open and he was nearby, she might stumble right into him—

The torch beam stabbed on again.

Shelby saw it dimly, nowhere close . . . no longer aimed into the woods, she thought. She sucked in a moist breath, groped around on the other side of the pine; nearly tripped again as she stumbled past another loom-ing tree trunk. Where was the lane? She couldn't be more than a few yards away from it . . .

Two more steps, and her foot splashed down into the runoff stream.

She waded through, felt the blacktop under her feet again. Out in the open again. The rain seemed to be slackening; the sting of the wind wasn't as strong now. But she still couldn't see anything except for the whitish shaft off to her right, pointed away from where she stood. Unless she'd lost her bearings completely he was back near where the cruiser was parked—

Another light, a *second* light cut through the darkness.

She blinked, blinked again. Definitely two flashlights now, one shaft bobbing up and down and side to side, the other stationary for a few sec-onds, then moving toward the other until they converged. *Two* men, both on the blacktop beyond the cruiser. Spectral shadow shapes, each pinned by the other's light. Thirty or forty yards away, too far for Shelby to see their faces through the rain.

She edged out farther onto the lane, moving sideways, feeling her way along. Still a long way to the highway . . . too far to try walking or even crawling blind along the blacktop. But what else could she do?

The two figures remained motionless up there, outlined by each other's torches. Talking, arguing—one of the lights kept moving in an agitated fashion. Their positions were such that she could no longer tell which was the newcomer, which was the one who'd been stalking her.

She couldn't keep standing there. Move!

The estate fence, she thought.

It paralleled the lane for part of the remaining distance to the high-way, she remembered, with only a few yards of separation on that side. Tall grass, an occasional tree, some shrubbery, otherwise nothing between fence and blacktop until the lane made a sharp inland bend. If she could get over there without being seen, she could pull herself along the boards . . . blind travel by the braille method.

The quickest way to the fence was a crab scuttle on all fours; if she tried to get there standing up she was liable to lose her footing, blunder into something, make noise that might carry over the diminishing wind. She dropped and began to crawl, weight on her forearms, hands brushing through the storm debris. Her cold fingers tingled, anticipating the end of the blacktop and the touch of the high, wet grass.

Sudden flare like a camera flash.

Faint popping noise.

One of the flashlight beams jerked skyward, pinwheeling, then dropped straight down and extended outward—an elongated yellow streak along the littered surface of the lane.

Gunshot! One of them shot the other!

Shock held Shelby rooted for two or three seconds. Urgency released her, propelled her forward, scrabbling at the lane now, her head turned toward the two figures. The one still standing swept his light over the mo-tionless form of the other, over the pavement nearby; then the beam fore-shortened as he bent or knelt, probably to make sure the one he'd shot was dead.

He took his victim's torch, too: One bolt of light reappeared, followed by a second. Both swung around in Shelby's direction, then steadied into wavering parallel lines.

Before either one found her she was off the lane and into the high grass, wiggling through it flat on her belly, her arms making awkward swimming motions in front of her. One sweeping hand encountered an obstruction; she detoured around it, but so close that part of whatever it was plucked at her raincoat, cut painfully into her cheek.

The flash beams separated, one probing the woods, the other swaying back and forth along the lane. Coming closer.

The fence, it couldn't be much farther—

There! One hand touched it, then her forehead bumped solidly against one of the vertical stakes.

The nearest light flicked away from the blacktop, hunting through the grass not more than a few feet behind her.

She found a chink between two boards, used it to lift onto her feet. Hung there for a moment to steady herself. The direction she wanted to go was where the light was; she had no choice but to pull herself away from it. Three steps, four, and all at once she was out of the grass and onto pavement again. But she hadn't lost the fence; one of her nails tore on the splintery wood—

No, not on wood . . . on a rounded projection of metal. Her gloved fingers traced over it, identified it.

Hinge, gate hinge.

The entrance gates. If she could get over them . . .

The one light was almost directly behind her.

She groped ahead of it to the joining of the two gate halves, searching for a foothold so she could make the climb. But in the next second she discovered she didn't need a foothold, she didn't need to climb—the halves were joined together but not locked.

She yanked them apart and plunged through.

TWENTY-THREE

Ir's TRUE," CLAIRE LOMAX said. Her eyes were open now, rounded, the pupils dilated and the whites that sickly clabbered-milk color in the fireglow. "I don't care who knows it now, I don't care what the police do to me if I live through tonight. It wasn't the Coastline Killer who shot Gene, it was Brian. And not down the coast, in our own living room. Brian, Brian, Brian!"

A sick metallic taste had formed in Macklin's mouth. He said, "For God's sake, why?"

"He blamed it all on me," she said. Talking to herself now as much as to him. Her gaze had shifted away, was fixed on something only she could see. "But it's not my fault, it's his, *his*. None of it would've happened if he hadn't started treating me like a . . . a toy he was tired of, a piece of useless baggage. I was faithful to him until then . . . I swear I was, I never even looked at another man. But you can only stand so much. That's why I had the affair, to get back at him."

"Decker? He's the one you had the affair with?"

"I didn't have any feelings for Gene," she said, "I never even liked him very much. But he'd been after me for a long time and finally I just . . . I let it happen. Twice, that's all. Only twice."

"How'd your husband find out?"

"I don't know how he found out . . . something Gene said, the way he kept looking at me with that smarmy smile of his . . . I don't *know*. But

Brian knew and he kept on hitting me until I admitted it. He wouldn't listen when I told him I was sorry, just hit me some more, then sat up most of the night drinking and brooding. Paula must've heard us, that's why she left. Brian accused Gene after she was gone. Gene laughed at him and Brian hates to be laughed it, he went and got that fucking gun of his, but Gene the stupid drunken fool kept right on laughing. You won't use that, he said, quit playing Dirty Harry, he said, and Brian . . . Brian . . ."

She shuddered, hugged herself before she went on. "Afterward he put the . . . the body in Gene's car and made me take it down to that rest area so it would look like the Coastline Killer did it. All that way with Gene dead beside me and Brian just ahead so I couldn't get away, so he could bring me back here and beat on me some more."

It had been Claire driving Decker's Porsche Monday afternoon, grinding the gears because she was scared or unused to a stick shift. He hadn't heard the SUV because Lomax, leading, had already passed by.

"Threatened to kill me too if I didn't do what he told me, if I didn't lie to the police when they came. But he's going to do it anyway—I knew he would, I knew it. He's crazy, he'll kill anybody who gets in his way . . ."

Shelby!

What if Lomax went all the way to the highway and she's still there and he finds her, tries to stop her from bringing help?

Another chilling thought jolted Macklin.

What if *Lomax* was the Coastline Killer?

TWENTY-FOUR

THE ESTATE DRIVEWAY SLOPED downward, flanked closely by timber on the south side. The darkness here wasn't quite as impenetrable as it had been on the other side; Shelby could make out the faint luminosity of frothing waves and high-flung spindrift below and to her right, and that the north side of the property was mostly treeless, the land folded into a long, deep crease. Half-seen tree trunks flicked past like black ghosts as she staggered ahead. The nyctophobia kept nibbling at her mind, radiating panic that threatened to send her into a disastrous headlong flight. The fight against it, the effort it took to move at a retarded pace and trust to the feel of pavement under her feet, had pushed her near the edge of exhaustion.

Had he seen her come through the gates?

No lights behind her yet. Maybe he hadn't—

Yes, he had. One beam appeared, then the other, splitting the night with short and then elongated streaks.

Without thinking she lengthened her stride. One foot slid on something yielding; she lost her balance and went down awkwardly, jamming her left knee this time, scraping more skin off her right palm. Pain flared and ran hot up into her crotch as she slid, then rolled half onto her side. She had to dig fingers and elbows into the sloping blacktop to check her forward momentum.

Neither of the shafts had found her yet, but they were drawing closer. Any second now.

The skidding fall had torn a long slit in the front of her raincoat; the oil-skin flapped like loose skin, got in her way as she tried to stand. She fought free, finally gained her feet, biting down hard against the throb in her knee, and flung herself off the driveway into the timber.

She hobbled between two trees, up close against another. The bared part of her hand touched rough bark, softer, thicker, stringier than on the pines by the lane . . . redwood bark. Mixed growth in here, pines and red-woods. She grasped a handful, pulled herself around behind the thick trunk a couple of ticks before one of the beams swept past.

There was more spacing between the trees here, and less ground cover. Ink-black in among them nonetheless, with only blips from the traveling lights to keep her oriented.

The thought crossed her mind that she'd trapped herself by coming onto the estate grounds. No other choice, he'd have caught her outside the fence if she hadn't—but unless she found a place to hide he'd catch her even more easily in here.

Jay—

But she couldn't help him unless she saved herself.

She groped her way blindly through the trees, dodging or plowing through obstructions, her knee still giving off shoots of pain, the muscles in both legs quivering with fatigue. Not thinking at all now, functioning on adrenaline and a savage determination not to give in to the fear.

The terrain kept sloping downward . . . toward the estate buildings? Had to be; the big, weirdly shaped house she and Jay had seen from the beach had been backed by woods. The rays crisscrossed behind her, moved up alongside, then out in front: Her pursuer must still be on the driveway. Shelby ducked as one flicked past, steadied, drew back. He'd seen her . . .

But he hadn't. The beam circled like a predatory bird seeking prey, slid off to hunt elsewhere.

Down, down . . . and at last she was on level ground. The spaces be-tween the trees seemed even wider now, nothing underfoot but wet, spongy earth. No place to hide in here. The trunks were tall and straight and impossible to climb in the dark. No chance of escape unless she could get to the buildings—

Ahead there, to the left . . . what was that?

Another light?

Yes! Below, not behind. Pale, unmoving, fuzzed by the rain. Beacon in the night.

Shelby sidestepped another tree, then two more, and finally she was out of the grove, coming into a broad clearing. Vague bulky shapes loomed ahead and to her left. The massive one farthest away was the estate house, the nearest, small and squat, an outbuilding of some kind; that was where the light was coming from.

Somebody was here, help was here . . .

She ran toward the stationary light, away from the moving ones.

Slipped once, almost fell again. For several strides she was back on pavement—the driveway—and then off it again onto more rain-soaked ground. From there she could see that the beacon light was leaking out through a window and a half-open door in the front wall of a small, square cabin.

As she neared it another stationary shape materialized beyond the pale yellow glow, touched by its outer edges.

Parked car. Escape, help for Jay.

Shelby hobbled to the doorway, caught hold of the jamb. Started inside with a cry forming in her throat.

Dying in her throat.

What came out instead was a half-strangled moan. She stopped dead still, sucking air, staring in at the floor.

A man lay sprawled next to the table that held an oil lantern, face down, motionless—a man wearing the uniform of a sheriff's deputy. Arms drawn together behind his back, wrists bound with duct tape . . . ankles, too. Blood from a wound on the side of his head gleamed blackly in the saffron glow.

Reflexively she took a step toward him. The holster on his Sam Browne belt was unbuttoned and empty. His head was half turned toward her, so that she saw his face clearly in profile—a face she recognized. Ferguson, the mustached deputy they'd encountered in Seacrest that first night, who'd showed up at the cottage yesterday with the highway patrol investigator.

But if Ferguson was here, hurt, tied up, then who had dragged her out of the cruiser, who was chasing her? And who was the second man who'd been shot?

Panic tore at her again. Run, get out of here before it's too late!

She turned away from the door. And froze once more, with the fear congealing inside her.

It was already too late.

TWENTY-FIVE

MACKLIN DONNED THE HEAVIEST sweater he'd brought, then sat on the edge of the bed to pull on wool socks and lace up his shoes.

"What're you doing?" Claire Lomax had followed him, stood in the bedroom doorway with a hand at her throat.

"What it looks like—getting dressed."

"Why? For God's sake, you're sick, you can't leave here—"

"But that's what I'm going to do."

"With no gun and Brian out there? You must be out of your mind!"

Maybe he was. But the bad feeling he'd had since she told him Lomax had murdered Gene Decker kept getting worse. Prodding him, filling him with a sense of dire necessity. Shelby might be perfectly safe, alone at the highway or in somebody's car on the way for help by now, but there was just as much chance that she wasn't; that Lomax had gone out that way hunting his wife. If he found Shelby instead, there was no telling what he might do. Coastline Killer or not, he was unhinged and unpredictable.

"Maybe so. But I can't keep on sitting here doing nothing," Macklin said. "He's out there and so is Shelby."

"What about me?" Claire's voice had risen to that hysterical edge again. "You can't leave me here alone."

"Come with me."

"No! I told you, he'll kill me if he finds me, he'll kill both of us if he finds us together—"

"Then stay here with the door locked."

"He'd break it down."

"Hide somewhere else then. One of the sheds behind the carport . . . he won't think to look in there."

"I couldn't stand it, trapped in a place like that. Please, please, I don't want to be alone."

He finished tying his shoes, stood up in slow, measured movements. Shelby had left the bottle of nitroglycerin pills on the bureau; he slipped it into his pants pocket. Claire clutched at his arm as he moved past her into the hall and he could smell the sweaty, fetid odor of her terror. He was sorry for her, but he couldn't do anything for her if she refused to cooperate.

She trailed him to the utility closet behind the front door, stood watching him paw through the shelves by candle flame. No other flashlight in there. The closet on the porch? Yes . . . on a lower shelf among a bunch of canned goods. But it stayed dark when he thumbed the switch; the batteries must be dead.

There was a package of D batteries in the utility closet. He grabbed his raincoat and hat from where Shelby had hung them, threw the coat around his shoulders as he went back to the living room. Claire was in his way; he pushed her aside, not roughly, but the contact made her flinch and moan.

He found the batteries, dropped the dead ones out of the flashlight and shoved in the replacements. Held a breath when he thumbed the switch this time, released it hissing between his teeth when the bar of light stabbed out. He shut it off, then quickly buttoned himself inside the coat, pulled on his gloves, yanked the hat down tight on his head.

Claire plucked at his arm, pleading with him again not to leave her. He said, "I'm going. You'll be better off coming with me."

"No, I can't go out there, I tell you, I *can't* . . ."

"Then go to the woodshed. Take one of the knives with you."

Macklin picked up the fireplace poker. Take the other knife along, too? He decided against it; he'd have to carry it in his coat pocket and it was liable to get hung up in the cloth. He might even accidentally stab himself with it.

He went to the door. A feral sound came out of Claire; she ran after him, dug her fingers into his arm to try to hold him back. He pulled away from her, flipped the dead bolt with the hand holding the flashlight, eased the door open a crack.

"Last chance, Claire."

"No!" She flung more words at him, called him a son of a bitch and something else he didn't listen to, and then he was outside.

Immediately the door banged shut behind him and he thought he heard the bolt slide home. He had a fleeting moment of concern for her. But she was beyond his help now. Shelby was his main worry, his only worry.

He stood studying the darkness, not thinking about Claire Lomax anymore. No light of any kind visible from here. The storm had lost some of its wildness; the wind had died down to intermittent thrummings, the rain to a light, misty drizzle. Even though it was well after nightfall, it didn't seem quite as cold as it had earlier. The boom and crash of the surf was all there was to hear.

His throat and mouth were dry, otherwise he was all right. A voice in his head reminded him that it didn't make any difference how he felt or thought he felt, he could still have another attack any minute. But he could drop dead waiting in the cottage, too. Anybody could suddenly drop dead any time . . . coronary, stroke, massive cerebral hemorrhage. You could get run over by a car or break your neck in a fall. You could get shot by a lunatic. If he didn't survive tonight, at least he'd die doing something important for the first time in a long time—die a man instead of a helpless invalid.

He made his way to the open gate. Visibility was poor—he could barely see where he was going—but he wouldn't put the flash on until he made sure Lomax wasn't roaming somewhere in the vicinity. He groped out past the carport, careful of his footing. Down the short drive to the half-flooded lane.

Still no lights anywhere.

He turned right on the lane, holding the poker down along his right leg, the flashlight in his left hand. The torch was necessary now or he'd run the risk of stumbling over something, hurting himself in a fall. He aimed the lens down at his feet, flicked it on and held it so that the pale yellow blob was no more than a yard ahead of him, just far enough to pick out obstacles to be avoided.

The Prius was parked close to the fallen tree. Macklin detoured around it, playing the flash over the pine's trunk and branches, looking for a way to climb over that wouldn't require too much effort. One place toward the upper end looked manageable, but when he tried it, a branch heavy with decayed cones snagged his coat and forced him to back off. He found a different spot, tried that. Another dead branch broke under his foot as he stepped up and over; he saved himself from sliding onto the splintered end by digging the tip of the poker into wet wood.

When he was down on the other side, he leaned back against the bole to rest. His pulse rate had climbed with the effort and there was a tightness like a contracting band inside his chest. Not now, he thought, not now! Slow, shallow breaths. The tightness didn't get any worse and there was no pain. A minute, two minutes . . . and his heart beat more slowly, the clamping sensation eased.

He made himself slog ahead at the same pace as before. The light picked out a torn-off pine bough six or seven feet long lying half on the lane, half in the stream of rainwater that gushed alongside it. He side-stepped the bough, into a gradual left-hand curve, and when he was halfway through that the outer reach of the shaft touched something else in the roadway.

It was just a shapeless lump until he closed the gap and the light brightened on it, gave it definition. Macklin pulled up short. Not an object—a man. Lying crumpled there, one arm outflung as if it were pointing down the lane. He took two more steps and then he could see the bare head, the rain glistening on the pink scalp visible through the close-cropped hair.

Lomax.

Fell, hit his head, knocked himself out?

Cautiously he moved up close, around the huddled body. The light was on Lomax's side-turned face then—on the open eye staring up blankly into the drizzle, on the gaping hole in his throat.

Christ! Dead. Shot, from the look of the wound. Dead for a while, long enough for the rain to have washed away most of the blood.

Macklin shook his head to clear it. Shelby? he thought then. Ran into Lomax here, he pulled that gun of his and there was a struggle and it went off? That must be it. And after it happened she must've continued onto the highway—which meant she was all right, she hadn't been hurt.

He almost turned back. Lomax was no longer a threat to Shelby, or to him or Claire; there was no reason to continue risking cardiac arrest out here in the rain and cold.

But then he thought: If that's what happened, where's the gun? It wasn't anywhere near the body, and when he moved Lomax enough to shine the light under him, he didn't find it there either. Shelby wouldn't have taken it with her . . . she wouldn't have any reason to with Lomax dead.

He lifted the light off the body, fanned it around and then moved farther along the blacktop. The appearance of the car parked beyond the jog surprised him almost as much as finding Lomax's corpse. He took a few steps toward it—and the torch beam glinted off the bar flasher on the vehicle's roof.

What was a sheriff's cruiser doing here?

Macklin went ahead to the cruiser, ran the light over it and through the side window. Empty. He made a three-sixty sweep with the torch: no sign of anybody in the area. Maybe Lomax hadn't died in a struggle with Shelby, maybe he'd been shot by a deputy . . . but then where the hell was the deputy?

He tried the driver's door, found it unlocked, jerked it open and poked his head and the light inside. And when he saw what lay on the passenger side of the front seat, his breath caught, his heartbeat jumped and stuttered.

Shelby's purse.

TWENTY-SIX

H E COULDN'T MAKE UP his mind what to do with the woman.
Or with the deputy.

So much weird shit happening all of a sudden, coming at him from different directions the way it had in that desert hellhole halfway around the world. Everything quiet, smooth-running since before the holidays, nobody bothering him so he could go on about his business unmolested, and then . . . bam!

Started to get weird when he found that guy dead in the Porsche down the coast—shot in the head and left on that overlook by somebody else—and had to beat it out of there quick before one of the police patrols came along. But that was nothing compared to all the heavy-duty crap that'd gone down tonight. First the deputy showing up, then the woman, then that drunken bastard up on the lane—one, two, three, out of the storm, out of nowhere, all in less than a couple of hours. It was like being ambushed by mongrel-dog snipers, the ones that came at you from door-ways and basements and collapsed buildings when you least expected it.

He'd handled it all so far, the way he'd handled the snipers in Iraq. You did what you had to do to protect yourself, stay alive. You blew them away.

Except that he didn't want to do that to the woman and the deputy. The guy up on the lane hadn't given him any choice, ranting like a buck-wild recruit and then pulling a sidearm, for Chrissake, forcing him to use the Glock, get in the first kill shot. React or die. Justifiable self-defense. But these two weren't armed and they weren't his enemies. Blow them away and he'd be guilty of murder, and he wasn't a murderer. Soldier on a mission. Preservationist. But a cold-blooded psychopath? No freaking way.

Oh, he could try to rationalize it. Threats to his safety . . . popping them was just another kind of self-defense. Like that afternoon in Baghdad when he and Charley Stevenson had been on patrol in what was supposed to be a secure neighborhood; were about to recon an abandoned store, watchful as always but not watchful enough because all of a sudden Charley's head exploded. Standing right there next to him, blood and brains and bone splinters flying everywhere. He didn't remember going into the store, just being in there and flushing the two civilians, middle-aged guy and a kid in his teens, no weapon in evidence but no question one of them had fired the burst that killed Charley, so when the pair started to run he'd burned them both. React or die, the officers drummed that into you from the get-go and you never forgot it. Only that time, in his dead-check afterward, he'd found an empty Tabuk assault rifle that made his kills righteous. Mongrel-dog snipers, two and out.

The pair of insurgent soldiers he'd shot in the firefight weeks later had been righteous kills, too. For a reason, for a purpose. Same here with the kid polluters in the sleeping bag and the drunk molesting the three sea lions and the clear-cutting caretaker and the abalone poacher. And with the loony up on the lane a few minutes ago. Justified.

The woman and the deputy wouldn't be. Not righteous no matter how much of a spin he tried to put on it.

Still, what else could he do?

He couldn't just leave them here trussed up and hit the road. Somebody'd find them, or the woman would find a way to work herself loose. They'd both seen his face, they could identify him. And the deputy had seen the car, could identify that, too. He wouldn't get far even if he picked up a different set of wheels.

Besides, there was still work to be done. Not along this part of the coast anymore, he'd have to move on no matter what and that was a damn shame because he loved it here, really loved it, it was the first place that'd ever felt like a real home. But there was more pristine coastline up north—the Lost Coast, the whole length of Oregon—and just as many spoilers to be dealt with up there.

The woman was saying something to him again. He looked over at her sitting on the edge of the lumpy brown sofa in her torn raincoat, hands and face scratched and blood-marked, legs pressed together and fingers gripping her knees. She looked wet and miserable and she had to be scared, but she didn't show her fear. He felt sorry for her. It wasn't her fault she'd got herself snagged up in this craziness tonight, any more than it was his.

"I'm not lying to you," she said for the second or third time. She'd started talking to him in a low, steady voice as soon as he sat her down and had kept it up ever since, saying pretty much the same things over and over—that she was from the cottage next door and she'd been out alone in the storm because her husband had had some kind of attack and she couldn't drive out for help because a tree had blown down and was blocking the road. "If he doesn't get medical attention soon, he could die."

Medical attention.

Flashback. Sudden and bright white the way they always came to him, like when a rocket exploded and lit up the night sky: *Men down, soldiers and civilians dying all around him from the roadside bomb. Blood everywhere, bodies and body parts torn up like butchered meat. Medic! Medic!*

The scene flared out. He rubbed his eyes, and he was seeing the woman and the room again.

"I'm sorry," he said, "there's nothing I can do for your husband."

"So what, then? What're you going to do to me?"

"I don't know yet."

"Kill me?"

"I don't know," he said.

She was quiet again, but not for long. "How long have you been here?"

"On the coast? Six months."

"Not living in this cabin the whole time?"

"No. The last two and a half weeks. Campgrounds, mostly, before that. But I needed a place for when the weather turned bad."

"Whose cabin is it?"

"Caretaker. Old man who was clear-cutting trees so the owners could have whitewater views. I hate that kind of crap."

"Where's the caretaker now?"

"He's dead." And buried in the woods behind the cabin. Always clean up your messes.

"Did you kill him?"

He didn't say anything.

"You killed the man on the lane tonight."

"That wasn't my fault. He was acting crazy. Waving a gun, yelling something about his wife. Didn't leave me any choice."

"Brian Lomax," she said.

"Who?"

"He owned the house at the far end."

Another neighbor. He hadn't even known he had neighbors until tonight. Well, once he'd gone out on the platform behind the estate house and he'd seen lights in the big place up there, but he'd never seen the people. Never given them any thought. He'd spent most of the past two and a half weeks forted up right here. Pretty spot even with all the old-growth trees along the crease clear-cut down to stumps; that was why he'd decided to squat here for a while, and most of the necessary provisions had already been laid in by the old man he'd buried in the woods. He'd only left the property a few times, for long drives along Highway 1 and once to buy some stuff he needed in the store in Seacrest.

"You shot all those other people, too," she said. "The Coastline Killer."

"I don't like that name. I'm not a murderer."

"You're going to murder me."

"I don't want to."

"Then let me go so I can get help for my husband."

"I can't do that."

On the floor the deputy twitched a little, moaned, but didn't wake up.

When he was quiet again, the woman said, "What happened with him? Why is he here?"

What happened. Come snooping around, that was what happened. Pushed his way in through the locked gates and walked down here through the rain with a flashlight and an umbrella, looking for the caretaker because somebody in Seacrest had mentioned not seeing the old man for a while. He'd claimed to be the old man's nephew, but the deputy wouldn't buy it. Suspicious looks, suspicious questions, then a sudden move for his sidearm. Not quick enough, though, not a well-trained soldier like he was. Easy enough to get the jump on him. He'd come close to putting a bullet in the deputy instead of cracking his head with the Glock. Why hadn't he? The uniform, maybe—the army taught you to respect a uniform, military or civilian. He wished now that he had popped the deputy, because at the time it would've been justified, another case of self-defense.

Couldn't shoot him after he was down, unconscious. Couldn't make himself do it. Tied him up instead, then took his keys and went up to move the cruiser inside the estate gates in case somebody came along. Just got the driver's door unlocked when he saw the woman's light; jumped quick into the woods before she spotted him. Would've stayed out of sight if she hadn't come right up to the cruiser, opened the door . . . he knew she was going to use the radio as soon as she got in. Couldn't just pop her, either, so he'd catfooted up and dragged her out. More damn hassle, then—a kick in the shin and an elbow in the gut and having to chase her around in the dark before and after that asshole with the sidearm, what was his name, Lomax, showed up.

It wasn't right, it wasn't fair. All this crap blindsiding him, screwing up his life just when he thought he had it on track and running smooth for the first time ever. No control over any of it, forcing him to take the kind of action he didn't want to take. A woman and a deputy and an armed head case. How could you guard against anything like that?

The Glock was right there on the table in front of him, three inches from his hand. The deputy's service revolver was in his coat pocket—he'd thrown Lomax's piece into the woods. Plenty of firepower . . . against a defenseless woman and an unconscious, duct-taped cop. Shit, man. Slaughter was all it would be. He might not lose too much sleep over killing the deputy, but doing the woman . . . that'd be the hardest thing he'd ever faced and he knew he'd hate himself for it later on. Never forget it, never forgive himself.

Maybe he should buy a little more time to come to terms with it. Bind her hands and feet, too—he hadn't done that yet, hadn't touched her at all—and then do what he'd intended doing before, go up and move the deputy's cruiser inside off the lane before any more crap went down.

"You didn't answer me about the deputy."

"Never mind the deputy."

"How long has he been here?"

"Why?"

"Whatever his reason for coming, he must've notified his dispatcher where he was headed. They'll be looking for him when he doesn't report in."

"Not right away. Not on a night like this."

"Before too long, though. And when they do they'll find his cruiser."

"I know that."

"Then you also know you can't stay here. The sooner you leave, the safer you'll be. Why not just go now?"

"And leave both of you here alive."

"Why not? We haven't done anything to you. By the time we're found, you'll be long gone."

"You know what I look like."

"Like any one of ten thousand young blond men—"

"No," he said, "I'm different. Easy to recognize, no camouflage. A soldier never jeopardizes himself or his mission if he can help it, and that's what I'd be doing."

"What mission are you on?"

"To keep the enemy from destroying what God made."

"What enemy?"

"Spoilers of nature," he said. "The ones who turn beautiful places into wastelands. They don't deserve to live."

"I'm not somebody like that. Neither is my husband. Or the deputy."

He looked at the Glock, looked back at her. "I almost wish you were."

"Why? Because that would make it easier for you?"

Smart, clever, but she wasn't fooling him any. All her talking was cal-culated to distract him, her eyes flicking here and there when she thought he wasn't looking straight at her, searching for something she could use against him, a way to get free. Wasting her time. The cabin was just two rooms, three if you counted the tiny kitchen, and there wasn't much in it; the old caretaker had lived a pretty lean life. Only a few sticks of fur-niture, bare walls, bare floor. There was a hunting rifle in the bedroom closet, but he'd unloaded it when he moved in. Fire tongs on a rack next to the woodstove, but she was too far away to get her hands on them quick enough and she was smart enough to know it.

He really did feel sorry for her. Liked her, too, because he could tell she had a soldier's kind of courage. The way she'd fought him up there on the lane, not making a sound the whole time, as hard to hang on to as a bagful of cats. And when he'd caught her down here . . . no screaming or crying or begging, no fuss of any kind. Just accepted the situation and was dealing with it the best way she knew how, the way a trained soldier would. Calm and cool under pressure.

He'd always admired that kind of courage in women. It was one of the reasons he'd fallen in love with Georgia . . . main reason, maybe. Georgia wasn't pretty, didn't have a great body, but she'd been a hell of a soldier and she had the guts of a lion. He'd rather have her as a battle buddy than 95 percent of the men in his Third Infantry unit. They'd done some hot and heavy loving over there in her CHU, really making the bed in that trailer rock, before she lost an arm in a firefight in Fallujah and they'd shipped her back home to Fort Bliss.

A dozen times he'd e-mailed her at the VA hospital but she never an-swered even once, just cut him out of her life without any kind of expla-nation. PTSD, probably, like he and so many other combat soldiers had suffered and would go on suffering. He'd tried to find her after they gave him his medical discharge and sent him back stateside, but her relatives in Oklahoma City wouldn't tell him where she was and he hadn't been able to track her through anybody else he talked to. She hadn't died, he'd've been able to find out that much if she had, so that was something to be thankful for. He hoped she'd rehabbed by now and was getting on with her life, wherever she was. She deserved some peace if anybody did.

He wondered if he'd've married Georgia if things had turned out differently in their part of the damn war. Probably not. He wasn't husband material. Too unsettled, too much of a loner. Needed to go places by himself, see things he'd never seen before, like California and the Pacific Ocean, get as far from the heat and filth and death-stink of Iraq as he could. That was why he'd come here. Clean sea air, unspoiled beauty. Calm, peaceful. Running on tracks along the edge of the world.

The woman was saying something else now, something he didn't catch. He said, "What?"

"How long are you going to make me suffer?"

"I'm not trying to make you suffer."

"But that's what you're doing."

"I'm sorry."

"Don't keep saying you're sorry. I don't want to die, I don't want my husband or the deputy to die, but if you're going to shoot me, why don't you just go ahead and get it over with?"

His head had started to ache. A dull throbbing centered behind his eyes. He squeezed them shut and knuckle-rubbed them, then dug the heels of his hands hard into his temples.

"Well?" she said.

Opened his eyes again, quick, but she hadn't moved. "I don't like this any more than you do."

"But that's not going to stop you, is it."

"I don't know yet," he said. "I don't *know*!"

And he didn't, he still didn't. It was like being back in Iraq, having to make another in a string of hard and fast decisions in order to survive. He'd handled it all right on the first tour, no problem, but on the second, after Georgia lost her arm and Charley got wasted and he had to scrag those two Iraqi civilians, it got harder and harder. To the point where he didn't know what was right and what wasn't, didn't know what to do, didn't want the responsibility, just wanted it to be over and done with one way or another.

He'd felt bad then and he felt bad again now. Harder and harder. Too much responsibility. Made him feel the way he had when they stuck him in that clinic over in Iraq—as if he'd lost part of himself, the way Georgia had lost her arm. And that it didn't really matter what he did tonight or from now on, shot the woman and the deputy or didn't shoot them, shot any more of the spoilers or not, because there was no way he could ever get it back.

TWENTY-SEVEN

H E WAS NOBODY SHELBY had ever seen before. Somewhere between twenty-five and thirty, lean and muscular, with a round baby face and thin blond hair wet and tangled from the rain. He didn't look dangerous; he looked like the boy next door all grown up. There wasn't enough light in the cabin for her to get a clear look at his eyes, but his expression—flat, almost placid—was not that of a homicidal lunatic. He didn't talk or act like one, either. Soft-voiced, except for flashes of anger that lasted for only a few seconds. Hadn't touched her or even come close to her, just ordered her to sit on the sofa and then sat down himself at the table across from it. Seemed almost apologetic each time he said he didn't know yet what he was going to do about her and the trussed-up deputy.

The Coastline Killer. She'd realized that must be who he was as soon as he caught her and now he'd confirmed it. Hiding out right here the whole time she and Jay were at the cottage. The Coastline Killer on one side and another violent weirdo, Brian Lomax, on the other. Sandwich meat between two slices of crazy.

Shelby kept trying not to look at the silver-framed automatic on the table in front of him, but her eyes were drawn to it mothlike. He'd killed a bunch of people already with that gun, for some warped reason that had to do with preserving the coastal environment, and pretty soon now, when he worked himself up to it, he would add two more to the list.

She was terrified, but she had the terror tamped down under the calm she had learned to adopt in crisis situations. If she let him see any sign of fear, it might be the impetus he needed to go ahead and use that automatic. All she could do was keep him talking, try to postpone it as long as she could while she continued to look for some miracle way to prevent it from happening.

She kept chafing her hands together to try to restore circulation; she'd stripped off what was left of the torn and sodden gloves when she first sat down. The cuts on her palms and her cheek stung like fury. But the rest of her felt numb, stiff from the wet and the cold. She had to clench her jaw muscles to keep her teeth from chattering.

The blond man's eyes were downcast now, in a squint that ridged his forehead with horizontal lines. Again Shelby made a surreptitious eye-sweep of the cabin. There was a wood box next to an old-fashioned wood-stove, some sticks of cordwood stacked inside. Maybe, if she could get him out of that chair and closer to her . . .

"It's cold in here," she said. "The fire's almost out and I'm freezing."

He didn't respond. He was massaging his temples again, as if he had a headache.

"Maybe you could put some more wood in the stove?"

"No."

"Or let me do it—"

"No. You just stay where you are."

No use. The cut logs were ten feet away, the deputy was on the floor between her and the table, and any sudden movements she made were bound to be clumsy. As soon as she came up off the lumpy sofa, he'd have the weapon in his hand—and one or two seconds after that she'd be dead.

Ferguson's limbs spasmed again, but his eyes remained shut. She hadn't gotten an answer to why he was here, what had happened between him and the blond man, but it didn't really make any difference. Even if his arms and ankles weren't bound, he'd be of no help to her or to himself. Nasty head wound—blunt force trauma, probable concussion. Likely he'd be so disoriented when he regained consciousness he wouldn't even know his own name.

Another groan brought the blond man's eyes back up. They flicked over Ferguson, lifted to resettle on her.

She said, "I don't know your name."

"It doesn't matter."

"I'd like to know. I told you my name."

"Shelby Hunter. I like that, it's kind of appropriate."

"Why appropriate?"

"The Hunter part, I mean."

"I'm not a hunter. I don't like to kill living things."

"Neither do I, but sometimes it's necessary." Then he said, "Soldiers are hunters, that's what I meant. Were you ever a soldier?"

"No."

"You could've been. You've got the courage."

She ignored that. "I'm an EMT."

"Medic? That's good. Can't do without medics."

"It's how I know my husband needs medical attention. If I hadn't been there to stabilize him after his heart attack, he might've died then."

"You told me that before. I'm sorry."

"The deputy needs attention, too," she said. "Why don't you let me look at his wound?"

"No."

"Maybe there's something I can do for him—"

"I said no."

Shift to another subject. Soldiers, the military.

"What branch of the service were you in? Army? Marine Corps?"

"Army infantry."

"NCO?"

"What else? I made corporal."

"Serve overseas? See combat?"

"Iraq, two tours," he said. "I hated it over there."

"I can't imagine what it was like."

"No, you can't. It was hell. But once you're there, all you can do is embrace the suck."

"Do what?"

"Make the best of it. Deal with all the shit until you . . ." His voice trailed off; he shook his head. "I don't want to talk about Iraq."

Keep him talking about something!

"Where are you from?"

"Nowhere," he said.

"You were born someplace, grew up someplace—"

"It doesn't matter."

"Do you have family? Brothers, sisters?"

"No."

"What about your mother and father?"

"I never knew him and the old bitch is dead." He was becoming agitated; his voice had risen, taken on a sharp edge. "There's no point in asking me all these questions. It won't work."

"What won't work?"

"Trying to distract me. You can't overpower me and you can't get away."

"I know that. I wasn't trying to distract you—"

"Don't lie to me. I don't like to be lied to."

"All right."

Silent stare for several seconds, his face showing the bunched effects of his headache. Then abruptly it smoothed; he pushed his chair back, picked up the automatic, and got to his feet. Resolute expression now, as if he'd made some kind of decision. Shelby tensed, but he didn't turn the weapon in her direction; held it straight down along his side.

"Lie down," he said, "on your belly."

"Why? What for?"

"Do what you're told, medic."

"Are you going to shoot me now?"

"Not if you obey orders."

There was nothing else she could do. She pulled her legs up and stretched out, slowly turned over with her cheek against a cushion that smelled of dust and mildew and pipe tobacco. A bullet in the back of the head, execution style? She resisted the impulse to close her eyes.

He said, "Put your feet together and your hands behind your back."

No, that wasn't his intention, not yet. He was going to tie her up as he'd done the deputy. She released the breath she'd been holding, let the prayer that had come into her mind slide back out again.

"Now don't move."

She obeyed while he tore off pieces from a roll of duct tape, wrapped her wrists together crosswise, then bound her ankles.

"Why are you doing this?" she said.

He didn't answer until he was finished and he'd tested the tape to make sure it was secure. "I have to go out again for a little while."

"Where?"

"It doesn't matter."

"But you'll be back."

"Yeah, I'll be back."

"And then what?"

"I don't know yet. Be quiet now, just be quiet."

At the periphery of her vision she saw him walk across to the door, open it, then stand there looking back at her. His face was impassive in the lantern light, but he had one more thing to say to her, oddly, almost shyly, before he went out and shut the door behind him.

"My name is Joseph," he said.

TWENTY-EIGHT

MACKLIN DIDN'T KNOW WHAT to think.

As far as he could tell, nothing had been taken from Shelby's purse; her wallet was inside, the unopened can of Mace tucked into a side pocket. Logic blocked the notion that there'd been a pair of cruisers and Shelby and the driver of this one had left together in the second. A deputy might have abandoned his vehicle if it was disabled in some way, but he'd sure as hell have locked it first. And Shelby would never have willingly abandoned her purse, not for any reason.

Something bad had gone down here, something that accounted for Brian Lomax being dead. The possibility that Shelby might also be hurt made him frantic. But no matter what had happened she was alive, he refused to think otherwise. Around here somewhere, or out by the highway. Alone? Lomax's body had been left where it had fallen; there was no reason for Shelby to've been taken away, hurt or not. Unless . . . hostage? No, no, what would anybody need a hostage for? She *had* to be in the vicinity.

He started to back out of the cruiser, stopped when his gaze rested on the pump-action shotgun in its console brackets. He didn't like guns, hadn't had anything to with any type of firearm since the time his father had taken him out hunting quail in his early teens, Pop's one and only effort to "make a man out of him." But in a situation like this you did what was necessary, whatever was necessary.

Desperation gave him the strength to tear the shotgun loose from its moorings. It was loaded: The slide worked smoothly and he heard a shell snick into the chamber.

The fireplace poker was useless now; Macklin tossed it into the runoff stream. With the shotgun crooked carefully under his arm, he swung the flash beam in a wide arc. It passed over the black woods, the deserted lane, the estate fence, the entrance gates—

He jerked it back when he realized that the gates stood partway open. They'd been shut all the times he'd driven by; he and Shelby had both assumed the place was closed up for the winter.

Was that where she was, somewhere on the estate grounds? The gates might have been blown open by the storm, but that wasn't likely since they opened inward. Somebody must've unlocked them . . . *somebody* was there or had been there.

Macklin hurried across the roadway, and as he sloshed through swampy earth and grass he had the presence of mind to click off the flash. He'd already thrown light over the gates, but anybody on the other side would have to be close by to have seen it. Possible someone was hiding there in the dark . . . he couldn't just go blundering onto the property with the flash on. Take it slow and careful.

He eased up to the nearest gate half, stopped there to peer through the gap. Thick darkness, unbroken except for the faint vertical outlines of trees—a dozen people could be hiding within twenty yards of him and he wouldn't be able to see any of them. He put a strain on his hearing. Magnified faucet-drip from the waterlogged branches, the distant pounding of surf. No other sounds.

He stepped through, took a few steps forward and felt the driveway begin to slope downward. He might be able to follow it down through the woods without using the torch, but he was afraid to risk it. Too easy to veer off, stumble and fall . . . hurt himself, bring on another cardiac episode. His breathing was a little off again and the squeezing sensation had returned. There was a growing numbness in his hands and feet, too— the bitter windchill penetrating the layers of clothing and robbing him of body heat.

He had the flash pointed straight down, his thumb on the switch, when the light flickers showed below.

Now he knew for sure someone was on the grounds. Moving in or beyond the timber on the south side, where he judged the estate buildings to be. He stood tensed, watching, as the flickers lengthened and then steadied into a long shaft. Whoever it was had moved out from behind the screening trees, probably onto the driveway, and was heading this way.

Before the shaft cut around in his direction, Macklin backed up quickly to the gates and then went to his right along the fence. Some kind of scraggly ground cover grew along it; he trampled through the vegetation, his shoulder brushing the rough boards, his shoes sinking into a soggy cushion of pine needles.

The approaching light was slanted upward now, not quite piercing the darkness as far as the gates.

Shelby?

But the hope died as fast as it had been born. She'd be running or at least hurrying, and judging by the rate the beam was advancing, whoever held the torch was maintaining a steady pace but in no real hurry. Going where?

A thick pine trunk jutted a few feet to Macklin's right; he pushed off the fence and stepped over to use the tree as a shield. His heartbeat had quickened and the metallic taste was back in his mouth. The stock and barrel of the shotgun had a heavy, leaden feel in his gloved fingers.

Two choices. Step out when whoever it was reached the gates, click on his flash, catch the person by surprise. Or stay hidden and try to see who it was, where he was headed.

No-brainer. He still had no idea who had killed Lomax—Shelby or the missing deputy or some unknown third party. Or why Lomax was dead. Or what the situation was here. He'd be the one at a disadvantage if the light-holder was armed and dangerous. He had no experience with a shotgun; to use it he'd have to take the glove off his right hand, and his fingers were cramped and without much feeling as it was. He'd be a damn fool to even think about trying to fire it one-handed while holding the flashlight steady on his target.

He bent forward against the pine trunk, watching the wavering ray draw closer, reach up to splash brightness over the gate halves. A single figure took dim shape behind it, slowed and then stopped to pull one and then the other half wide open. There wasn't enough backspill for Macklin to get a clear look at him. But he could tell one thing as the man and the light passed out through the opening: What he was wearing was not a deputy sheriff's uniform.

Macklin waited half a dozen beats. Snippets of light coming through chinks between the fence boards told him that the man was moving across the lane toward the parked cruiser. But he wasn't planning to leave the area, head for the highway; he wouldn't have opened the gates all the way if that was his intention. Must be going to bring the cruiser back inside, hide it on the estate grounds.

Was he the one who'd killed Lomax? If so, then wouldn't he also want to get the corpse off the lane? Put it into the cruiser or drag it into the woods where it wouldn't be easily found? That would take time, and so would stopping to close the gates after he drove the cruiser through.

Hurry!

Macklin stepped out to the rain-slick driveway, eased along it several paces in the dark while he altered his grip on the torch, closing his fingers around the bulb end and splaying them over the lens. When he switched on, enough light leaked through on a downward slant to show him what lay directly ahead, let him lengthen his stride. Every few steps he glanced over his shoulder at the gates. If the cruiser's headlights appeared before he reached the end of the driveway, he'd darken the torch and get off into the trees as fast as he could.

His breathing was still erratic; he kept expecting the chest constriction to erupt into smothering pain. But he didn't let it slow him down. Finding Shelby was all he let himself think about.

The driveway's looping descent had almost cleared the woods when he saw, first, the yellowish rectangle ahead to his left and at almost the same time, the brighter illumination tingeing the night above and behind him. But the cruiser's headlamps were still outside the fence, just now swinging around to the entrance. He couldn't make out the gates from where he was, but the buildings had begun to materialize ahead, the dark outlines of the big estate house on the edge of the bluff and the smaller, closer structure with the lamplit window.

The driveway forked; he veered onto the left fork, drawn by the light ahead.

Halfway there, he took another look beind him. Headlight glare showed through the trees . . . moving at first, then becoming stationary. The cruiser was inside the gates and the man had gotten out to close them. Only a matter of minutes before he'd be down here.

The small building was a rough-built cabin. Macklin stumbled and slowed as he neared it, his breath like fire in his lungs. He passed a closed door, brought up next to the unshaded window. Sleeved his eyes clear of rain and sweat and peered through the streaked glass.

Jesus!

He lunged sideways to the door, dragged it open just long enough to thrust his body inside. On the battered gray sofa Shelby's head came up and her eyes rounded into an open-mouthed stare. She cried his name, twice, in a voice that cracked with emotion.

Relief flooded him. She wasn't hurt, she looked all right.

"Thank God, Jay, but how did you—"

"No time now. He's coming, he'll be here any minute."

"Quick then . . . get a knife, cut me loose."

Macklin sidestepped the wounded deputy—recognized him, Ferguson—and stumbled into the kitchenette. Didn't have to open drawers to find a knife; there was a wooden block of them on the sink counter. He exchanged the flashlight for a long-bladed carving knife, stumbled back out to the sofa.

His hand was shaking so badly he was afraid he might add another cut to Shelby's already torn and bloody flesh if he tried to slice through the duct tape one-handed. He propped the shotgun against the sofa, stripped off his right glove, then held the knife in both hands to steady it as he steered the blade to the narrow gap between her wrists.

As he began sawing, she said with awe in her voice, "You came all this way on foot? Miracle you made it . . ."

"I'm okay."

Damn knife blade was dull; he sawed harder. Nicked her in his haste—a line of fresh blood slithered along one wrist.

"Is he on foot or in the cruiser?"

"Cruiser."

"Pray he doesn't notice the shotgun's missing, it'll put him on alert."

"Who the hell is he?"

"Coastline Killer. Hurry, Jay!"

One more cut and her hands were free. She took the knife from him, sliced the tape around her ankles, then reached for the pump gun. He tried to take it from her; she said, "No, let me have it, you're in no condition," and came up off the bed with it in her hands. She looked shaky, but not as shaky as he was.

He said, "Shell in the chamber," and she nodded. She knew how to handle the weapon; you couldn't do emergency work around cops for ten years without having seen a riot gun being used.

Rising sound of a car engine outside. Headlight glare slid obliquely over the front of the cabin, across the window.

Shelby said, "Get out of the way, Jay, over by the stove."

He didn't argue. His tank was almost empty; he'd been running on scant reserves for some time now. He shoved himself upright, made it over to an old armchair by the wood stove and leaned heavily against its back, straining to get his breathing under control.

Shelby moved past the deputy to the right side of the room, at an angle to the closed door; stood there with the shotgun leveled, her legs spread and her hands steady now. Frozen tableau for half a minute. Then the door opened and a blond man Macklin had never seen before came inside. Hadn't noticed the pump gun was missing from the cruiser, hadn't been put on alert, just walked right in.

The blond man saw the empty sofa, stopped abruptly at the same time Shelby said in a sharp commanding voice, "Stand still, soldier! I'll blow your head off if you don't do what you're told."

He stiffened, staring at her with surprise on his wet face; then the surprise shifted into tight-lipped anger, then into something else for a second or two, then to no expression at all. His posture seemed to turn even more rigid, into a military erectness—both arms flat against his sides with the still-burning flashlight pointed at the floor, shoulders drawn back, chin up, eyes straight ahead and unblinking.

Shelby ordered him to unbutton his coat, take it off and let it drop on the floor, then to lie facedown on the sofa, hands behind his back, feet together. "If you don't obey orders, you're a dead man. I mean it, Joseph." Then she said something Macklin didn't comprehend. "I've got a soldier's courage, remember? And you know soldiers don't make idle threats."

"I know," the blond man said. Just that, nothing else.

The round boyish face was still expressionless. Macklin, exhausted, not tracking too well anymore, thought that he must have misread what he'd seen there before the blankness set in.

It had seemed almost like relief.

EPILOGUE
NEW YEAR'S DAY

THIRTY-SIX HOURS NOW, every one a blur.

Shelby sat in the waiting room at Santa Rosa Memorial Hospital, drinking coffee to stave off fatigue and remain alert. As far as she knew Jay was still in the OR—it seemed like he'd been in there half the day. The head staff surgeon who was performing his bypass operation had been cautiously optimistic. Jay's coronary had been relatively mild; the damage to his heart didn't seem to be as severe as it might have been given his night prowl through the lag end of the storm. But any number of things could go wrong during major surgery, and there was always the chance they might find further blockage that hadn't been revealed by the tests.

That kind of thinking wasn't making the wait any easier. She made an effort to blank her mind, or at least to shift it into a state of semiawareness. No good either way. The concern for Jay kept intruding. So did the dulled memories of Wednesday night.

Some of the details of what she'd endured between the time of Jay's heart attack and his arrival at the cabin had already begun to fade. She'd been over them so many times she'd lost count, with various law officers and the first wave of media vultures, and yet it was as if it had all happened months ago. A form of mental self-protection, she supposed. The more awful an experience, the quicker the mind sought to bury it under layers of scar tissue.

The rest of that long night was a little clearer in her memory—for the present, anyway. A time of organized chaos. Douglas's term for an intense Saturday night in ER. (Douglas. Her feelings for him still uncertain and unresolved. But this wasn't the time to be thinking about them. Or about anyone except Jay.)

But yes, organized chaos was just what it had been. Jay holding the shotgun and telling her how he'd found her while she taped Joseph's wrists and ankles. Joseph lying with his face turned away from them, as docile as if he'd been drugged . . . no, as if he were a resigned prisoner of war who wanted as little as possible to do with his captors. Helping Jay out of his wet clothes, then getting him comfortable in the bedroom while she checked his vital signs. Using the radio in Ferguson's cruiser to report the situation and ask for medical assistance. Cutting the semi-conscious deputy loose and tending to his head trauma as best she could. Finding out from Jay that it was Brian Lomax, not Joseph, who'd killed Gene Decker; that Claire was hiding somewhere in or near the cottage, and why. Waiting for what seemed like hours, but was only about thirty minutes, for the Basic Life Support ambulance operated by the Seacrest Volunteer Fire Department to arrive, along with a caravan of sheriff's department and highway patrol officers.

Watching a bundled-up Jay and the wounded deputy being whisked away toward Fort Bragg in the BLS ambulance because the weather was still too poor for a medevac helicopter to land at Seacrest. Answering a seemingly endless string of questions before one of the deputies finally drove her to Fort Bragg. By then the BLS ambulance had rendezvoused with an Advanced Life Support ambulance at Albion, Jay had been hooked up to a cardiac monitor and had an IV started and been fast-driven to Mendocino Coast District Hospital, which had a landing pad that allowed helicopters to land even in stormy weather, and then transferred by Reach 1 to Santa Rosa Memorial's cardiac care center.

Another string of questions for her at the Fort Bragg sheriff's office. An interminable two-hour car ride to Santa Rosa. New rounds of Q&A with the staff at SR Memorial, with Lieutenant Rhiannon at the local highway patrol office, and then, briefly, with the members of the media swarm she wasn't able to avoid. Four hours of restless sleep in a motel room, all she could manage despite her exhaustion, and back here to the hospital for more waiting.

One long continuous blur. It was a wonder she could remember any of it, think clearly at all.

If Jay came through the surgery all right—and he would, he would—the worst was past. Something else was past, too, or she was pretty sure it was: her fear of the dark. If that hellish night hadn't cured her nyctophobia, nothing ever would.

But it would be a while before the authorities and the media let them alone. She hadn't looked at TV or read a newspaper, but she could imagine the headlines: SOUTH BAY COUPLE CAPTURE COASTLINE KILLER AFTER NIGHT OF TERROR. She didn't want any part of it, and she was sure Jay wouldn't either, but like it or not they were temporary celebrities. It wouldn't last long, though. This kind of thing never did. There was always a new and different piece of sensationalism for the newshounds and the public to feed on.

She got up to use the bathroom. Came back, wondering if she could stand to swallow any more coffee—and the surgeon, still in his scrubs, was waiting for her. The small tired smile he wore told her everything she needed to know.

Everybody kept telling Macklin he was lucky to be alive. Shelby, the North Coast EMTs, an ER doctor at Santa Rosa Memorial, the surgeon who performed his triple bypass surgery. As if he needed confirmation of the fact. Nobody knew it better than he did.

But he was thankful for an even greater piece of luck—that he'd had enough stamina to do what he'd set out to do, that Shelby was alive and unharmed. One of the nurses called him a hero for risking his life to save his wife's. Bullshit. Heroes were cut from a whole different variety of cloth than Jay Macklin. The kind of cloth Shelby had been made from—she was the real hero here. He was just a man who'd finally stepped up, finally proved to himself—and if he was lucky, to her—that he wasn't a failure or a loser after all.

Shelby was there with him before he went into surgery, and at his bedside when he came out of the anaesthetic in ICU, but not when he woke again later, more or less clearheaded, in a private room. That was because his surgeon and a nurse were there instead; she was waiting outside. They'd let her come in as soon as they were done checking him and the tubes and monitors he was hooked up to.

How was he feeling? Like I just lost a long race with a turtle, Macklin thought. But all he said was, "Okay." The surgeon had told him in ICU that the operation had gone well, but in case the patient had been too groggy to understand he repeated it again now. All his vital signs were good. Barring any unforeseen complications, he should fully recover and be able to lead a normal life.

Normal. Meaning average, ordinary, reasonably sane and moderately productive. He'd settle for that, all right; he'd hang on to it with both hands and never let go.

They left finally and let Shelby come in.

So pale and tired looking . . . but she was smiling, and for him the smile was as much life support as the tubes and monitors. There was so much he wanted to say to her, but the first words that came out were inane: "I guess I'm still lucky, huh?"

"So far so good." She drew a chair over close to the bed and sat down. "You look a lot better than you did Wednesday night."

"Didn't think I was going to make it?"

"On the contrary. I knew you would."

Little white lie, so he told one to match. "Me too."

"The doctor said ten minutes, then you need to rest."

"Ten minutes . . . How's Ferguson?"

"Severe concussion, but he'll be all right."

"Claire?"

"They found her hiding in the woodshed at the cottage. Pretty badly frightened but otherwise okay. As far as I know she's still in custody, but I don't think they'll bring charges against her."

"Better not. It was all Lomax's doing—he deserved what he got."

"That seems to be the general consensus."

"They find out who the blond guy is?"

"Joseph Marshall. Army corporal, served two tours in Iraq. Halfway through the second he had a stress-related break. Spent time in a combat stress clinic, then was given a medical discharge. I guess the army doctors didn't realize how seriously disturbed he was or he'd never have been released."

"Another casualty of that fucking war."

"And five collateral casualties—six if you count Lomax. Marshall hasn't confessed to any of the shootings yet; he's not talking to anybody. Name, rank, and serial number."

Macklin's eyelids were growing heavy from the painkillers and other drugs they were pumping into him. "Getting sleepy already," he said. "There's something you have to know and I better get it said while I'm still coherent."

"It can wait until later—"

"No, it can't. Too important. I'm not the same person I was before we went up to Ben's cottage."

"Neither of us is," Shelby said.

"Not at all in my case. I know why I've been so closed off most of my life, why I kept shutting you out. It's all explained in that nightmare I kept having. My subconscious finally puked it up after the heart attack."

He told her about the nightmare, in detail, and the words came easily. "It always embarrassed me," he said, "one reason I could never talk about it. Kid's fantasy monster. Only it wasn't a fantasy. Distortion of something that actually happened when I was a little kid, six or seven."

"Repressed childhood trauma?"

"That's it. My mother and Tom were away visiting my aunt; I had a cold so I was left home with my father. Loud night noises woke me up and I went down the hall to see what they were. My old man . . . he was in bed with a woman he must've sneaked into the house after I was asleep. One-night stand, or somebody he'd been cheating on my mother with all along . . . no way I'll ever know. They were screwing, but I had no idea that's what I was seeing. In my kid's mind it got twisted into something a lot more horrible."

Shelby said, "A monster feeding on something still alive."

"Right. I must've made a noise because he saw me, reared up off the woman, and started yelling. I ran and he chased me, caught me trying to hide in my bedroom closet, dragged me up by one arm—must've felt like the arm was being torn off. I was so scared I peed all over myself. What he was screaming at me . . . my subconscious turned it into whispers because the words were too terrifying. Something like 'Forget what you saw tonight. You ever tell your mother or anybody else I'll rip your fucking head off, I'll chew you up like hamburger.'"

"My God. Six years old . . . no wonder you repressed it."

He was starting to lose focus, to drift and fade. He said quickly, "The fear he put into me built a mental block: Don't ever confide anything to anyone, keep it all locked away inside. But the block's gone now, I'm done hiding."

Shelby didn't say anything. Still skeptical.

"Give me the chance," he said, "I'll prove it to you. Will you?"

The nurse picked that moment to come in and call for an end to the visit.

Shelby got to her feet.

Macklin gave her a pleading look. "Will you?"

"Heart melter," she said softly.

"What?"

"Never mind. I'll think about it."

". . . I love you, Shel."

Almost under now, his eyelids so heavy they wouldn't stay open. He didn't see her face when he heard her say, "Yes, I know."

A NOTE ON THE AUTHOR

Bill Pronzini is the author of more than seventy novels, including three in collaboration with his wife, the novelist Marcia Muller, and is the creator of the popular Nameless Detective series. A six-time nominee for the Edgar Allan Poe Award (most recently for *A Wasteland of Strangers*), and two-time nominee for the International Association of Crime Writers' best novel of the year, Pronzini is also the recipient of three Shamus Awards and the Lifetime Achievement Award from the Private Eye Writers of America. He lives in northern California.